THE DEATH OF BOYS

The Death of Boys

by

Gary Fry

Black Shuck Books
www.BlackShuckBooks.co.uk

First published in the UK by Black Shuck Books, 2018

978-1-913038-10-6

Carole had taken on additional work because she needed the money. The problem was that although her boss had sent her office files an hour ago, her ageing laptop was unable to open them. She had little patience with technology, but had nobody around to help. Even her son knew more about computers than she did, but he was away with his dad, camping in the Yorkshire Dales.

Carole reopened the email and clicked on its attachment. The dropdown menu displayed the contents, but when she tried accessing them, nothing happened. The screen simply said, "Files failed to unzip" – whatever *that* meant.

She rose from the dining table and crossed for the kettle. She wouldn't mind a glass of wine, but with Harry to take to school tomorrow and an early start at the office, it wasn't worth the risk. Instead she made coffee, wondering what she could tell her boss about the files.

The best option was to be honest, but she didn't want him to think her incompetent. There might be more overtime in the future, and if she did this assignment well, it would help show that she could be trusted to work from home.

After drinking half the coffee, she returned to her laptop and tried opening the documents again, but received the same infuriating message: "Files failed to unzip".

Maybe her boss had made an error before sending them; it mightn't be her fault at all. At any rate, this gave her an excuse to ask him to resend them. Nick, the estate agency's manager, was a decent man, and although there were complications between them (he'd recently asked her out for a date and she'd refused), he'd proved understanding about her circumstances and how these affected her work.

After sending a brief email, her mobile phone rang. She plucked it out of her pocket and examined the screen: it was Neil, probably telling her what time he planned to bring their son back. It was the first time Harry had been away with his dad and stepfamily (Stella, the new wife, and her two boys, Kyle and Brad). Carole hoped he'd enjoyed it, because however much she loved him, she could do with more breaks herself.

She answered the call.

"Don't panic," her ex-husband said, with much the same contrite tone he'd used when telling her about his affair last year, "but something's happened…"

~

When Neil's car pulled up outside about an hour later, Carole hurried to open the front door. Tears pricking her eyes, she saw her boy advancing up the garden path, sweeping the beam of a flashlight ahead of him as if it was a laser.

"I got *zapped*, Mummy," he said with excitement. If what Neil had mentioned over the phone had caused serious damage – physical injury or mental shock – Harry didn't appear to show it. "The thunder roared in the sky, like a monster, and sent down a bolt to fry me!"

Although he seemed in good spirits about having been struck by lightning, Carole didn't care for the way he ascribed sentience to such a random event. She stooped to hug him and then pushed back hair from his forehead. The boy looked okay, but was it always possible to tell?

"Where did it strike you, darling?" Carole asked, swallowing emotion like a lump of dry bread.

"Right here," her son explained, twisting and pointing between his shoulder blades. "But it didn't hurt one bit. Kyle and Brad were *well* impressed."

Carole wasn't sure what she felt about Harry referring to his stepbrothers so enthusiastically but supposed she'd have to get used to this. After all, as her ex-husband had married Stella during the summer, there was no chance of her and Neil ever getting back together.

Still holding Harry, Carole noticed her ex-husband following on the path, lean frame looking dapper in casual clothing. She still felt bitter about what he'd done – splitting up the family, leaving their son to be passed around relatives – but realised that he couldn't be held responsible for this freak act of nature. Surely the important thing was that Harry was – or certainly seemed to be – all right.

"That must have come as a shock to you all," said Carole, feeling as awkward as she had each time Neil had collected their boy for his weekend visits.

"Not as big as the one *he* suffered," Neil replied, but the joke fell flat. Carole realised he must be nervous, too. It had been only a year since their separation.

Once their son had run inside, claiming to be "starving", the man spoke again.

"I couldn't believe it, Carole. It happened so quickly. There we all were..."

"All?" she asked, knowing who she meant but making him say their names anyway.

"Well, yeah. Me, Stella and the boys."

How cosy, she thought with bitterness. *How quickly your guilt was erased and you've got on with your new life.*

"...so there we were, just walking through the countryside," Neil continued, his considerable height leaving him aloof from her obvious unhappiness, "and then *bang*, Harry dropped like a stone."

"Why were you outside in such weather anyway?"

"It just came upon us unannounced. We were

actually heading back to the campsite after a long walk. It's weird how the lightning struck *exactly* where he was."

Again, she didn't like the way the event was described – not as a monster this time, but as something which had acted with intention. But she was fretting too much, the way she'd been forced to do lately.

After expressing worries about hidden impacts on Harry's health, Neil was able to reassure her.

"We took him to the nearest hospital. Stella insisted, actually. The other boys were really worried, too. Anyway, Harry got checked out and he's fine. Not even a punctured eardrum. They said that I...well, that *we* should keep an eye on him for a few days."

His correction had hardly helped Carole feel more comfortable; she gave voice to her concerns at once.

"You mean this happened *hours* ago? That your...your wife and even her kids knew about it? But that you didn't think to call *me*?"

"I didn't want to worry you, Carole. What good could it have done? I knew it was your day off work and you'd be resting." Neil, looming a foot above her, smiled with all the charm of his salesman occupation. "The important thing is that Harry's fine. Don't you agree?"

He'd always been able to talk himself out of awkward situations. Indeed, how could she respond negatively to his question when she'd thought much the same earlier?

Hearing her son rooting in the kitchen cupboards behind her, Carole said, "I'd better get him fed and then to bed. He has school in the morning. We'll talk about this later, Neil."

In response to her firm tone, her ex-husband looked defensive and even apologetic.

"Okay," he said, like a boy caught transgressing some petty rule. But then he brightened. "He won't need any food, though. I bought him a burger and chips on our way over. Believe me, he *demolished* them."

From behind, Carole heard cereal rattling into a bowl. If a strong appetite was the only symptom of his latest experience, she had nothing to worry about. As for other matters, particularly how Neil dealt with their son – well, she'd have to give that serious thought.

~

Once Neil had departed for his cushy new home across town, Carole checked out Harry's vision, hearing and heartbeat. These were amateur attempts to reassure herself that what her ex-husband had claimed a hospital medic had told him was backed up by her own observations. True to Neil's word, the boy seemed fine.

After tidying the chaos his appetite had inflicted on the kitchen, she considered not her son's physical health but any psychological issues which might arise from his altered family circumstances. Might dividing time between his parents cause long-term issues? Or could the experience be positive, helping him to mix with others and get what he wanted from life?

It was all very confusing, and after tucking him into bed that evening with just an hour's TV allowance before sleep, she tried to prevent things from getting on top of her.

"Did you have a nice time with Daddy?" she asked, standing at his bedroom door.

"Yeah, it was good," Harry replied, still holding the flashlight with which he'd come home. Carole imagined that Neil had bought this for him, which was just like his behaviour: flash-with-the-cash but rarely reliable on other matters. "We had yummy food and played games and went swimming in a river."

"That's nice," said Carole, trying to sound as if this was what she truly thought, despite feeling left out of it all.

Harry glanced at his TV burbling in one corner, but then returned his gaze her way.

"But it wasn't the same without you there, Mummy," he added, smiling his heart-breaking smile.

At that moment, Carole found herself having to step out of the room, switching off the light as she went, hoping the boy hadn't spotted her tears welling up.

"Goodnight, Harry. I love you."

"Love you, too."

~

Back in the kitchen in front of her laptop, Carole removed her glasses and wiped her eyes. Despite lingering worry about Harry, she must now focus on other matters. Refitting her glasses, she squinted again at her screen, checking to see if her boss had replied to her email.

He had indeed, explaining that he'd placed the documents he'd sent earlier in a "zipped-up folder", something Carole had never previously heard of. Nick, presumably guessing that her computer lacked appropriate software, had included a link below his message. She clicked on it at once.

After being directed to a website offering a free program to download, she removed her glasses again. She often suffered eyestrain while using a laptop, leading to regular headaches. She knew that better lenses were available – ones with non-reflective surfaces, cutting out screen glare – but couldn't afford to upgrade. She wished she didn't have to wear glasses at all, but it was something she had to live with.

A minute later, the program had installed, allowing her to try, for maybe the tenth time that day, to open the files her boss had sent. She got further this time, the folder yielding its cargo and transferring her to a new window. But then another message greeted her: "Insufficient memory available."

It was now nine o'clock; for the second time that evening, she felt like crying. She wouldn't be able to start on Nick's work, which would surely leave him unwilling to offer her overtime in the future, choosing other staff who lacked her complications.

Hands clenched with frustration, Carole shut down the laptop. She'd just wasted another hour of her weekend off and refused to sacrifice more. After reaching the kitchen doorway, she observed black marks scratched into its frame, revealing how quickly time passed. These indicated the height of her son recorded over the past few years at six-month intervals, each about an inch apart, with the last made only months ago. Christ, how soon before he was as tall as her? And how much more food would he eat then?

After switching out the lights and heading upstairs, she told herself that Harry's ravenous hunger this evening – consuming so much cereal after apparently eating fast food on his way home – was just a one-off impact of his experience earlier, the shock having a weird impact on his biology. All the carbs he'd devoured must be keeping him awake, because as she passed his shut bedroom door, she noticed light moving across the crack beneath it.

This couldn't be the TV, because Carole heard no accompanying sound. She recalled the flashlight with which the boy had arrived home. Harry must be still playing with this, pretending it was a laser, like in some of his favourite films.

She called through the door, telling him to switch off the light and then go to sleep. He obeyed her – the beam beneath the door vanished at once – and as she headed for her own room, she didn't dwell on the fact that her son hadn't called back a single comment.

~

The following day at work, Carole headed anxiously to her boss's office, feeling apologetic after failing to work on the files he'd sent the previous day. She explained about her computer problems, how the program he'd linked to hadn't helped, and said that she hoped this wouldn't prevent him from asking her to do more work at home in the future.

"Hey, don't worry," Nick said from behind his desk. "Those files weren't urgent – they don't have to go to the client till the end of the week. There's still time."

Carole took a seat opposite him. "Okay, thanks. But I'll probably have to do them here, on one of the office PCs. Because mine's kaput."

She wondered when she'd find time to do the work – after her office days she collected Harry from her mother's (where he went after school) – but then Nick leaned across the desk.

"Look, Carole, I have a proposition to make."

Oh God, she could do without this again. She liked her boss but wasn't ready for a new relationship.

But that was when he pleasantly surprised her.

"How about I come to your house one night this week and see if I can fix your computer?"

"Oh, I..."

"Look, no strings, okay? You made your feelings clear a while back and I respect that." He hesitated, running one hand across his balding scalp. "Anyway, I'm actually being selfish here."

"You are?"

"Of course. I mean, if I can get my most efficient staff member equipped with a PC, I'll be able to offer her more work at home, won't I?"

She smiled at that, inside mostly, and then rose from the chair.

"Thank you, Nick," she said, heading for the door, eager to repay the trust he'd shown by putting in a full day's work. But then, turning quickly, she added, "Can you make it tomorrow evening – about seven? That's when Harry and I tend to eat. You could…well, you could join us if you like."

When Nick smiled, Carole had to resist concluding that she'd just fallen into another man's trap. That wasn't a healthy way of thinking. She mustn't shut herself off from the world.

"Thank you, Carole, that would be very nice," Nick replied, his smile broadening. "I'll look forward to that."

"Me, too," said Carole, but moments later, after exiting his office, she wondered whether that was actually true.

~

"Has he been okay?"

She'd told her mum that morning about her son's experience over the weekend and asked her to observe any unusual behaviour on his part after collecting him from school.

"He's been fine. He's eaten half a packet of biscuits – he wanted more but I told him no, as you'll be having your teas later – and since then, he's been in the lounge drawing pictures."

Despite remaining concerned about her son's

appetite, Carole was eager to return home, hoping to locate at least something decent in the freezer for tomorrow evening's meal. She didn't feel uncomfortable about her boss visiting but was worried about other things, such as whether the house was presentable and what her son would think about another man in their home.

Heading into her mother's lounge, she recalled that Harry and Nick had met briefly one day in the office and that they'd got along well enough. Not that there was any reason why this was important. She and her boss were only colleagues, of course.

Her son, seated on the floor, was surrounded by sheets of paper. He also had a pack of pens beside him, from which he'd removed blue, green and black ones. Carole stooped to see what he'd been drawing. The first was like many she'd observed at home, land at the bottom represented by a block of green with offshoots like plants growing; the sky far above was as most children did it, a band of blue at the very top of the page. But there was a notable variation: the boy had left space above the sky, which was occupied by...well, how could Carole best describe the figures? The truth was that they looked like nothing which had ever occupied earth.

Mildly alarmed, Carole told herself that these were just a child's conceptualisation of birds erroneously assumed to survive outside the world's atmosphere. But which birds had ever boasted such boneless frames and so many clawed limbs, let alone a luminous vision depicted by beams spilling from the things' weird skulls?

"Harry? What are *these*?" Carole asked, pointing to the top of the drawing, her forefinger now shaking.

Her son glanced up, and just then a strange noise arose from inside him: his stomach gurgling. He must be ready for his tea.

"*Zappers*," said the boy, suddenly looking older than Carole was used to. "They're what *got* me from outer space, Mummy."

He then offered her other drawings, one showing a tiny figure standing upon another landscape and being struck by a jagged fork from the sky. A second sketch was of a faraway planet apparently communicating with earth via radio waves hinted at by unstable lines.

The boy smiled, but Carole didn't care for

that expression. It didn't touch his eyes. In fact, it didn't look like Harry's smile at all.

~

When she collected him from school the next day, Harry seemed more interested in a maths class he'd enjoyed than in far off astral bodies and any weird creatures lurking on the earth's fringe. He'd probably just being watching silly films again or playing noisy console games, with either or both affecting his imagination. At any rate, while cooking a meal she hoped not to feel ashamed of later, she dismissed all these concerns as symptoms of her recent anxieties.

Her boss arrived exactly when she'd asked him to. Nick had thoughtfully brought along a bottle of fresh fruit juice, from which Harry could enjoy a few glasses, too. When the boy joined them from his bedroom as Carole dished out a chicken dish, Nick expressed astonishment at how much he'd grown since they'd last met, maybe a year ago.

"Time flies," Nick said, ruffling the boy's hair. "You'll be as big as me before long."

Although this comment troubled Carole for some reason, she tried not to dwell on it as she sat alongside her two male companions.

"Do *you* have any boys or girls, Nick?" asked Harry, bright-eyed innocence supplanted by the hunger he displayed while snatching up his cutlery. "And if you do, where's their mummy?"

"Stop being nosy and eat your food," Carole said, despite realising that the boy might be simply trying to figure out how families worked, particularly fragmented ones. Then she turned to smile at her boss, who didn't look at all embarrassed and simply smiled back. Carole knew that Nick was divorced and had two daughters away at university. But that was irrelevant. He'd visited for just a simple meal and to fix her computer.

Once the meal was done – Harry had devoured a first and then asked for a second helping – Carole told her son to watch TV in the lounge while the adults focused on "boring work stuff."

"Goodbye, Nick," said Harry, cheeks plump with all the food he'd eaten. "I hope you come here again. That juice you brought was fab."

"You're very welcome, big guy," Nick replied, and as the boy exited the kitchen, Carole's gaze fastened again on the marks she'd made on the doorframe: her son's height recorded semi-annually.

But then her attention switched back to Nick.

Twenty minutes later, once they'd drunk some coffee and Carole had booted up her ageing laptop, Nick focused on what he'd come to do.

"Basically, your hard drive is crammed with data. It's impossible to save anything new onto the system."

She responded with a thin smile. "What does that mean in normal language?"

Her boss laughed, turning the screen in her direction and giving her no choice but to shuffle her chair closer to him.

"Put it this way, if this were a dustbin, stuff would be spilling over the top."

"That's probably all the photos I've stored," she explained, averting her gaze and then pushing her glasses up her nose. "They're all from...well, you know, the past. Family snaps, mainly."

"Sorry, I didn't mean to imply—"

"Don't be silly. To be honest, binning is all many are worth. So let's do that."

She was thinking of shots of herself with Harry and Neil, before her ex-husband had done his bunk. She wondered if there was a way of deleting them without having to view any. When she asked about this, Nick explained that he could minimise the photos' sizes, revealing all as just "thumbnail shots."

Carole shook her head. "Unzipping files... thumbnail shots... insufficient memory... No wonder I'm confused. It's a different language to me."

Nick laughed again, scrolling down a page of shrunken versions of old photographs – "Goodbye, tall guy, who didn't know how lucky he was," he said as the last image was consigned to oblivion – but then returned to Carole's email server.

"Zipping up files is a way of sending lots of information to another computer via an email attachment."

Still feeling flattered by his previous comment, Carole forcefully ruled out any connection between the words "zipping" and "zapping", and then said, "I don't get it. How is it possible to get more stuff inside the same sized container?"

"Try not to think of it as normal space," Nick explained while opening the files he'd sent a few days ago. "It works differently from things in the real world."

"Right," she said, but wasn't sure she understood. In fact, all she could now picture in her mind's eye were the drawings her son had executed yesterday, those strange things lurking on the rim of the world. But then she pushed aside this concern.

Once he was finished, Nick shrugged off her gratitude, saying that the meal she'd kindly prepared had been more than compensation for his efforts. Then he rose to leave. While passing along the hallway, he called into the lounge entrance, "Goodnight, big guy."

Harry called something back but failed to appear at the doorway. Carole didn't know what to make of that, but then Nick had turned to face her again.

"Thanks for a lovely evening." He hesitated a moment, holding her stare, and then added, "Perhaps we could—"

But she cut him off. "I'll work on those files and get them to you by the end of the week."

"Ah, yes." Nick straightened himself up, shoulders pushed back. "That would be great, thanks."

"You're welcome," she said, and then awkwardly let her guest out.

~

After quickly washing up, she took a pen from a kitchen drawer, crossed to the doorway and then called her son from the lounge.

Harry came at once, still panting after all the food he'd eaten this evening. A comment her boss had made earlier had triggered a concern Carole felt she'd been suppressing lately. When her son reached her, she elected to convert anxiety into action.

"Stand here, Harry," she instructed, manoeuvring the boy up against the doorframe.

"What are you doing, Mummy?" he asked, not resisting the way she handled him, even though he now looked capable of doing so. But then he realised what she was up to. "It's too early for this, isn't it? I thought we only did it at Christmas and near my birthday in July."

Ignoring him, she laid the pen flat on his head and then etched another mark into the doorframe. It turned out that this was over an inch above the previous one, which had been recorded in late-summer after her son had turned seven years old. At that moment she told him to go upstairs to change for bed. He complied with untypical obedience, leaving Carole alone with her discovery.

Harry had grown more in only a few months than he had during the previous six. But the most troubling thought of all was that this mightn't involve months at all. It might be just days.

~

She booked a doctor's appointment for the next day, her final one off from work this week. The previous day had felt awkward, she and Nick pretending that their relationship was restricted to the office. But Carole had busied herself with tasks, keeping her thoughts off her recent discovery of her son's sudden change in size.

After dropping off the boy at school and driving straight to the GP surgery, however, it was this issue which preoccupied her. She sat in the waiting room, reading a magazine article about single mothers until she was summoned by the PA system.

Dr. Lynch, reassuringly middle-aged, had been her physician for as long as she could remember, and his avuncular manner always made her feel comfortable. All the same, she felt reluctant to address the real issue she'd come to discuss. She began by mentioning the eyestrain she'd suffered lately, leading to bad headaches.

The man said he could prescribe an alternative to tears which would reduce dryness arising from staring too long at computer screens. If that failed to work, he recommended that she visit an optician to determine whether her vision had deteriorated and she needed new lenses.

"I'm fed up of wearing glasses," said Carole, straightening her frames to deflect the doctor's scrutiny.

"I'm afraid we're stuck with them," Dr. Lynch replied, adjusting his own thick frames. "Unless you're partial to wearing contacts."

"I've tried them. They make my eyes itch."

"Then how about corrective laser surgery?"

Carole flinched. "Oh no, I don't like the thought of that. Lasers in my eyes. *Ugh*."

The doctor laughed, as if he agreed, and then Carole judged it an apt time to change the subject.

"Actually, Doctor, there's something else I wanted to mention..."

When he leaned back to invite her to

continue, she felt confident enough to tell him what had happened to Harry the previous weekend, before describing the boy's uncommonly keen appetite since. Then she mentioned the most outlandish aspect of her concerns, the boy's sudden increase in height.

"You mentioned Harry's father," said Dr. Lynch, once Carole had drawn her edgy account to a close. "He's quite a tall man, isn't he?"

"Yes, about six-two." Carole felt stupid for not having considered this previously. "Do you think that's why Harry's growing so fast?"

"How old is the boy now?"

"Seven."

"Hmm."

Carole's eager glare prompted the doctor to continue. He did so obligingly.

"During the first year of life, children grow about a foot in height, but after that it's usually just a couple of inches each year."

"Yes, that was the case with Harry. I take a reading every six months. But the pattern has changed now."

Dr. Lynch stroked his chin. "Yes, it does sound unusual, but that's not the same as saying that it's unprecedented. I'm afraid I'm no expert in the area. As I suggested earlier, this may be a sudden growth spurt prompted by his genes. But I can't say for certain right now."

Carole nodded and offered a strained smile. "I understand that, Doctor."

The man perked up in his chair. "Let me make a few enquiries and see what I can find out. I'll contact you by telephone in a few days. Would that be okay, Mrs...forgive me, *Miss* Franklyn?"

It would have to be, thought Carole, standing to leave. Surely nothing serious could happen in just a matter of days.

~

She'd just reached her vehicle when her phone rang. She plucked it out of her pocket, privately hoping it might be Nick from the office, asking her to do more work at home or perhaps issuing a less impersonal invitation.

But it wasn't her boss. It was her son's school. One of Harry's teachers wanted to see her in person as soon as possible and wondered whether lunchtime today was convenient. Carole said she could make the appointment and then hung up.

What was so important that it required a face-to-face meeting at short notice? She'd find out by driving over there. After parking in a street alongside the school, she got out and advanced for the entrance.

The building's interior had an antiseptic aroma which put her in mind of authority. She'd always left formal engagements like this to Neil, but had lately had no choice but to take them on. Narrow corridors hemmed her in her like gangs of bullies. The many children she passed seemed to have more confidence than she did. She eventually reached the school office, where a receptionist asked her to take a seat before summoning the teacher Carole had named.

This woman, forty-something and solidly built, arrived a few minutes later, stooping towards Carole and proffering a hand which engulfed hers.

"Thanks for coming so promptly, Mrs. Harrison. It's appreciated."

"Sorry, it's Miss Franklyn now," Carole said, her tone unwittingly apologetic. "Harry has kept my ex-husband's name, but I've reverted to my maiden one."

"I see," said the teacher, who'd introduced

herself as Mrs. Davis on the phone. Then she led Carole into an office bearing only a table and two chairs. "Please take a seat."

Where was her son? Had something happened to him? Why was Mrs. Davis being so officious? Despite her concerns, Carole said nothing as she sat down. Long seconds seemed to pass before the woman, also now seated, spoke again.

"I wanted to discuss a sensitive matter with you, Miss Franklyn, and thought it wise to do so on a one-to-one basis. Nip it in the bud, as it were."

Carole nodded promptly, even though her heart rate had just accelerated. "That seems sensible, Mrs. Davis. But can you tell me what the problem is?"

"Certainly. It's presently a small matter, but we at the school are eager to prevent things from escalating and try to involve parents as early as possible."

"I'll do whatever I can."

"Okay, please let me explain." Mrs. Davis paused, leaned forwards with her elbows on the table, and then continued. "This morning in a maths class your son was rather disruptive. If this were a one-off incident, we'd tackle it without troubling you. But the truth is, Miss Franklyn, that Harry has been difficult all week."

Why did the woman keep mentioning her name, as if emphasising the "Miss"? Did Mrs. Davis consider her a stereotypical single mother with a problem child?

"What has he done?" asked Carole, forcing steel into her voice.

The woman held her stare. "An altercation has occurred with his maths teacher, Mr. Lucas. In a class concerning quantity, Mr. Lucas set the children a problem involving five pint-sized cups of water and a two-pint jug. He asked the group how many cups would remain full once the jug was filled and your son insisted that *all* could be poured inside the jug.

"Now, you and I know this is incorrect, but at this stage in children's lives, that doesn't concern us. What does, however, is wilful disobedience. When Mr. Lucas pointed out the error, Harry became aggressive. He thumped his table and threw stationery across the classroom. The other children grew frightened. All the while, your son insisted that his answer was correct. Do you understand the issue now, Miss Franklyn?"

Carole certainly did, but couldn't help feeling disturbed. This was so unlike Harry that it might be another boy.

After pushing hair from her face, Carole said, "Thank you for bringing this to my attention, Mrs. Davis. I should tell you that my son was involved in an incident last week, which has obviously affected him more than I thought. Can I ask permission to take Harry out of school today? That will help me address the problem."

"I've yet to mention his behaviour in the dinner hall yesterday..."

"As I said, if I can take him away with me now, I'll do my best to sort it out. He...he needs his mother."

The woman nodded, eyes suddenly softening. Perhaps she was a mother herself.

"That will be fine, Miss Franklyn. Take as long as you need."

~

"What's wrong, Harry?"

They were at their kitchen table, having just eaten boiled eggs and toast. Her son had asked for four eggs, but Carole had restricted him to one. This was partly punishment for misbehaving at school but also related to other concerns. The truth was that she was worried about his physical and mental well-being.

"I don't know, Mummy," the boy said, eyes full of tears which threatened to spill down each cheek.

"What do you mean?" She tried to make her voice sound simultaneously tender and authoritative. "What about what happened at school today?"

"*I can't even remember*," Harry said, with a little of the anger he'd apparently demonstrated in class lately.

"Okay, just relax, Harry." She reached out to grip her son's right arm, with which he'd just hit the table. "I don't want to fight. I just want to understand what's going on."

Had her son grown bigger still since she'd measured him only days ago? Glancing up at her, his face puffy with unease, he certainly looked different; eyes hooded and skin pale, as if he'd recently suffered a fever and had struggled to overcome it.

Carole took a deep breath and spoke again. "Was it getting so angry that made it difficult for you to remember what happened, Harry?"

"No, Mummy, it was weird. I felt really scared. When my teacher asked me about cups, I didn't know where I was. I even forgot Mr. Lucas's name. I know that now but didn't then. All the other children seemed different as well, as if I didn't know any of them. It was like they were...were..."

"Were what, Harry?"

"*Aliens*, Mummy. Like in that film I watched a bit ago, where lots of pods landed on earth and took over all the people in a town."

Carole, feeling frightened, recalled the movie her son meant, a black-and-white feature she'd enjoyed with him a few weeks earlier. Frankly, the games he played on his console seemed scarier, but was that necessarily true? Might the film's themes relate to what Harry was currently experiencing in his family life? Were his recent drawings attempts to communicate related concerns, using fictional ideas to illustrate deep psychological issues? In short, had Harry been trying lately to tell her something, and had she been too preoccupied by other matters – dealing with her ex-husband, taking on extra work, even developing a relationship with Nick – to notice?

Unwilling to push him harder at the

moment, Carole gave her son a hug and insisted that he go to his bedroom for rest. She watched him go with tears in her eyes. Then she marshalled her mind. She'd make an appointment for him at the doctor's, where she'd insist on more medical tests and, if necessary, a psychological assessment. The boy had disturbed her, especially with talk of incidents beyond what she might expect from a mere loss of temper. In the early days of her marriage, Harry's father had suffered mood-swings, after which he'd often claimed to be unable to recall what he'd said or done. Carole had always found this excuse unconvincing, but might he have been honest, after all?

She spent the rest of the afternoon browsing the Internet, exploring the symptoms her son had experienced lately. The after-effects of lightning strikes were apparently limited to physical impacts, like sensory impairment and cardiovascular irregularities. Carole knew that Harry had been tested for both in hospital and that no obvious concerns had been raised.

Carole followed links to other sites, most dealing with children's health. One suggested that at certain periods, hormonal changes could lead to rapid physical and mental developments. Did this mean that a sudden spurt of growth might be accompanied by psychological turmoil? Or were disordered thoughts more to do with the events in a youngster's life?

She found one site especially troubling. It suggested that divorce and fragmentation of the family could be challenging for children, particularly those with no immediate peers: siblings, close friends, adults to help explore their experiences. One potential outcome involved a split in the child's mind, as he or she sought to reconcile demands arising from different relationships. In some cases, this could lead to creative thought – many famous artists had experienced such complicated upbringings – but in others the results might be delusions and fantasy.

Carole closed down her laptop, hands now shaking. Suddenly all she could picture in her mind were airborne creatures with boneless frames and claw-topped limbs, each shooting light beams from their skulls where the eyes should be.

Zappers, she thought, and wondered whether she was in her right mind herself.

~

After she and Harry dined – he ate with unsettling haste, devouring enough pie and potatoes for two or more of him – Carole made two phone calls in private. The first was to Neil to ask whether the boy was still spending the weekend with him and his new family. When Neil said yes, Carole quickly outlined what had happened at school and asked whether Neil would speak to their son with a view to finding out what was troubling him. Neil, revealing concern and guilt at the same time, agreed at once, and then Carole hung up.

Her second call was to Nick, her boss, asking him if he'd like to visit for another meal while Harry was with his dad. Nick agreed at once, despite sounding surprised by the invitation. The truth was that it had surprised Carole, too. She guessed she'd just been feeling lonely, vulnerable, reckless, even pissed off. Why shouldn't she have something potentially good in her life? She was beginning to realise that she liked Nick a lot.

Later that night, while sleeping alone in her vast double bed, she was awakened by a sense of someone moving around the first floor of her home. She had an impression that lights were shifting beyond her closed bedroom door as uncertain footsteps shuffled in the hallway.

She must be dreaming. If that were Harry going to the bathroom while holding his new flashlight, why would *two* beams appear to be at play, each flicking back and forth with a fuzzy static sound?

Exhausted from the previous day's unrest, Carole closed her eyes and fell asleep again. She experienced no further disturbances that night.

~

Once she'd completed the files Nick had asked her to work on at home and submitted them to the office, Carole thought she might actually be able to enjoy the weekend.

There'd been no further incidents with Harry. On Friday, he'd gone to school and seemed to have had a problem-free day. Carole had talked by telephone to Mrs. Davis, and they'd agreed to keep the boy under surveillance for a short period, each reporting unacceptable behaviour if it arose.

As a reward for his improved behaviour,

Carole had, after work, picked up her son from her mother's and, with money from her overtime the previous evening, taken him out for a fast-food meal. Even though he'd chosen the biggest meal and then asked for dessert, Carole had wondered whether she might have overreacted to what (as some websites she'd consulted claimed) was quite normal during childhood: hormonal changes resulting in spurts of growth and leading to a need for greater sustenance. Unsettled thoughts, including imaginative fantasies, were probably just a symptom of that. As Dr. Lynch had suggested, Harry's dad was tall; perhaps the boy was simply conforming to his genetic profile.

After Neil collected Harry that Saturday, Carole's only regret was not asking Harry about his bizarre drawings. She'd had plenty of opportunities to do so, but had felt scared about what she'd learn and had pushed the issue to the back of her mind – not quite deleted, but certainly zipped-up in a mental folder.

Later that morning, however, a new concern arose. She'd entered her son's bedroom to search for the flashlight that was clearly distracting the boy, keeping him up late at night and maybe even making him tetchy at school. It wasn't on his bedside table, which was littered with sweet wrappers and crisp packets. Then she thrust her arms under the bed and pulled out what was closest to hand. Among this detritus was indeed the flashlight, but when she tried activating it, nothing happened. The bulb was dead, as if the batteries had expired.

Perhaps Harry had overused the device lately, but when would he need to? At night, perhaps, when the only other light was from stars beyond his curtained window? Despite the warmth of the house, a quick shiver rippled down Carole's back. Then she reviewed the papers she'd also removed from under the bed.

Here were more sketches, not unlike those Harry had made at her mother's house, but much darker and far more suggestive. One involved a human-shaped figure so packed with other entities – each bearing a boneless frame, angular limbs, and beams of lights bursting from their eye sockets – that it had grotesquely expanded to accommodate them. Another showed what resembled an amorphous mass bursting open to reveal innumerable other things – certainly none resembling creatures ever seen on earth – which then scuttled away, forging paths ahead with laser-like rays spilling from their weird skulls. In a third, a whole town appeared to have been torn apart by these newcomers, all its property reduced to rubble.

Dropping the pictures involuntarily, Carole stood and fled the room. Before she reached the staircase down, however, she froze on the spot, simply observing.

Several strips of wallpaper hung from the hallway, as if burnt off by a tool capable of generating vicious heat.

~

By the time Nick arrived later she'd calmed down, but still felt the need to discuss her concerns with someone she felt she could trust. As soon as she'd poured him a glass of the wine he'd brought, she told him about everything: the lightning strike, her son's new monstrous appetite, his freakish drawings, his apparent expansion in size, the strange light she'd spotted overnight, Harry's behaviour at school, the scorched wallpaper, and even allusions to alien life the boy had made.

It all sounded crazy presented like this, but

she'd been unable to help herself. It occurred to her that she might be experiencing some kind of breakdown, having failed to adjust to all the hurt Neil had caused by betraying her. Whatever the truth was, she certainly welcomed Nick's sudden embrace. She understood that he wasn't taking advantage of her, that he genuinely seemed to care. When they parted, he snatched a clean handkerchief from one pocket and handed it across.

"Thanks, Nick," she said, averting her gaze, as if her tears were something to be ashamed of. "I expect you think I'm a drama-queen, don't you?"

"Not at all, Carole," he said, displaying his usual tender smile. "I think you're obviously going through a difficult time."

Nick, divorced and with adult children, probably knew more about this than she did, but it wasn't the moment to dwell on unhappiness. He might feel as uncomfortable about his life as she currently did about hers. And anyway, she'd invited him over for a meal and was determined to enjoy it.

They ate pork and, after finishing the red, started on the white she'd had chilling in the fridge. Now that the alcohol had doused her worries, she'd started to relax in Nick's company. Did this suggest that there was more to this engagement than merely friends enjoying each other's company? Carole wasn't sure, but felt it would be foolish to rush into anything. After all, if her developing relationship with Nick didn't work out, it would make her job difficult.

After dessert, they moved into the lounge, where Nick asked whether she'd suffered any more computing problems. Carole said the laptop was running well, but then, feeling more able to address the matter now, she switched the conversation back to earlier concerns.

"I'm less worried about Harry's physical health – my mum always says that if children have a good appetite, there can't be much wrong with them – than about his mental well-being."

"How do you mean, Carole?"

Nick had spoken gently, both interested and non-judgemental. She felt encouraged to continue.

"Oh, you know," she said, tapping one temple with a finger. "What goes on up here. Psychological issues."

"Ah, I see." Nick thought for a moment, sipping more of his wine, and then spoke again. "Other than a few weird drawings and some youthful fancies, do you have any reason to believe that your son has suffered some kind of trauma?"

She shook her head. "I guess I'm referring to the divorce – his father leaving and all the rest of it. That's bound to have an impact, isn't it?"

"Yeah, I hear what you're saying. I certainly remember feeling similar when my own marriage broke up. But I was on the other side of it, having to leave without the kids. It was just irreconcilable differences with my ex. Anyway, for a long time, I feared that the girls might be scarred – you know, all the stuff we read about in the media."

Carole nodded, realising what he meant. Stories on TV and in newspapers were commonly sensationalised. Before she could respond, however, Nick went on.

"Believe me, it tends to work out. I mean, look at my daughters now: both at university and doing well enough. It's sad that things like this happen, but that's just life, isn't it?"

Carole considered these heartening words,

but even so felt troubled by them. At only thirty-three years old, she could be no more a decade older than her boss's daughters, while Nick, in his late-forties, was closer to her mother's age. In the event of a relationship with him, would any of this be a problem?

She was about to respond to his comment, even lean forwards to welcome a first kiss, when a car pulled up audibly outside. At first, she thought this couldn't have anything to do with her – the cul-de-sac was ringed with houses similar to her own – but when footsteps – multiple pairs, all making a hasty clatter – advanced up her front path and then voices were raised with rancour, she grew alarmed.

Ducking away from Nick, she stood from the couch. The room swayed a little as she headed into the hallway, but she somehow kept her balance. She was just about to snatch open the front door when someone did so on her behalf, and those voices grew noisier still.

Five people were gathered near her front entrance, all illuminated by starlight. She spotted Harry nearest the threshold, as if he'd been fleeing the rest. Directly behind him stood Neil, appearing torn between their son and the three people standing beyond him: Stella and her boys, Kyle and Brad, each of whom appeared outraged, faces white with shock.

"What is it? What's happened?" asked Carole, stooping to her boy. But Harry barged her aside with a strength she hadn't anticipated, before advancing into the property and mounting the steps, presumably headed for his bedroom.

Neil paced forwards, still looking uncertain about where his loyalties lay. When Carole glared at him, he eventually spoke.

"We were just returning from a restaurant," – he hesitated, turning to glance back at his new family, all of them continuing to express visible disapproval – "and then Harry, with no provocation – I mean, I'd say if there had been – well, he started saying all these *creepy* things."

"Creepy? What do you mean, Neil?"

Just then, Nick arrived behind Carole, placing a supportive hand on one of her shoulders. In response, Neil, who'd been about to add more about their son, hesitated and then visibly recoiled, as if surprised by the sight.

"Oh, this looks cosy," he said a moment later, during which he believed he'd figured out what was going on.

Carole, angered by Neil's hypocrisy, snapped, "Can you please tell me what Harry has done?"

She heard her son upstairs, heavy footfalls pacing back and forth as if he was full of rage. If his recent behaviour at school was anything to judge by, that was probably true, but before she could do anything about it, she needed to know what had happened on this latest occasion.

But after glancing again at Nick, all Neil could say was, "How long has this been going on? Christ, no wonder my son is so confused."

Carole sensed red rage mounting inside her. She glanced beyond her husband, at the woman on the path pretending to be affronted by whatever sticks-and-stones comment Harry had made to either herself or her precious brats. Then Carole looked again at Neil.

"You utter shit!" she cried, indicating his new family with one flaying hand. "You're the one who went off with them. You're the one who destroyed what we had together."

"Stop deluding yourself, love," Stella called from a few safe yards away. "Neil hadn't been happy for years. You just never saw it."

"Keep out of it, you bitch!" Carole yelled back, the alcohol making her lose rational grip.

"Don't you speak to our mam like that!" one of the two boys said, and then, with similar vehemence, the other added, "At least neither of us is a psycho like Harry."

"Just tell me what he's done!" Carole shrieked, causing at least one pair of curtains to twitch elsewhere in the neighbourhood.

That was when they all heard the explosion.

At first Carole assumed the sound had come from the sky, a vast black realm glittering with stars. But then she identified its actual source, and this was even more disturbing.

It was Harry's bedroom.

It had to be the boy's room because his window faced on to the front of the property, just above where she and her visitors were rowing. The noise – a savage thud accompanied by a hissing which escalated in volume, like snakes slithering to raise fattened heads from slimy bellies – had sobered her perception, forcing her to turn and hurry beyond Nick, before advancing up the staircase and finally reaching her son's shut door.

She hesitated there, listening carefully. The crackling electronic sound inside the room sounded like a great computer malfunctioning.

Innumerable lights batted to and fro beneath the door's lower edge. She recalled Harry's flashlight not working that morning, and then, with escalating horror, she wondered what the beams might be.

Quickly opening the door, she stepped over the threshold. Then she heard things being flash-fried inside, multiple strips of wallpaper removed from the plaster behind. Looking around, she saw nothing more than multiple beams of light, all projected from the heads of shadowy shapes standing in each direction, maybe twenty or thirty of them. Had these things responded to her arrival, moving bonelessly her way, their claws snagging on the carpet? Perhaps they planned to do to her what they were doing to their surroundings, lashing those multi-coloured lasers every which way. Carole heard furnishings being evaporated but was still unable to see what the creatures – *Zappers*, Harry had recently called them – looked like.

Despite so much activity around her, she refused to switch on the light. Her mind sharpened by trauma, she suddenly understood everything. With a single flash of lightning, compressed data had been transferred from space. Her son's memories had been erased to accommodate this new material. And now, with a sinuous rustle which spared her no mercy, countless intergalactic files were in circulation.

With a scream that lasted and lasted, Carole realised what must have been done to her boy to release the otherworldly entities which now rushed to silence her. Indeed, as she observed a wet shape on the bed, far larger than any child had any right to be, she didn't wish to observe how Harry had been unzipped.

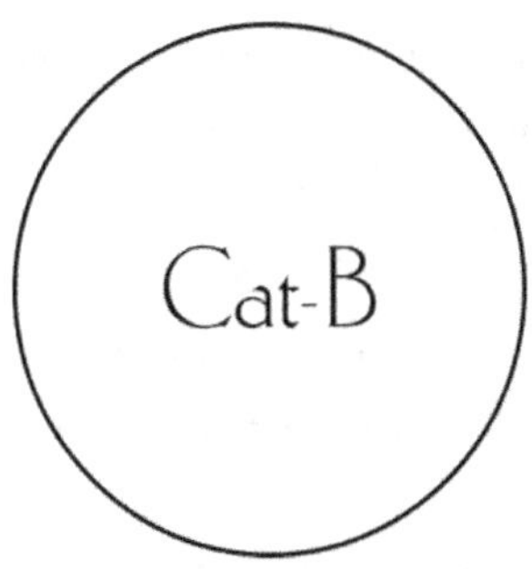

Jake was in his bedroom, struggling with A level revision, when his dad stepped through the doorway without knocking.

"Call for you," he said, passing over the landline handset. "Make it quick."

"Who is it?" Jake whispered, reaching out to accept the phone and then covering the mouthpiece with one hand.

Dad's face almost conceded an ugly emotion but somehow remained as professional as it had to be in his business. "It's him: *Harry*." – he spoke the name like a cat spitting or a bee delivering its sting – "Don't be too long. You've your maths to get through yet."

When dad left and shut the door, Jake sat up on the bed, glad to be free of the physics and chemistry he'd been studying this evening. He briefly wondered why his best friend hadn't called him on his mobile, but then realised that Harry would probably be out of credit again.

"All right, tosser," Jake said down the line, adopting the coarse comedic talk he believed was used by lads who went to schools different from his.

"You're gonna love me, mate. You're gonna...love...me."

Jake privately thought he already did – his newfound friendship with Harry had certainly lessened some of the tensions in his life – but it would be social suicide to admit anything like that.

"Tell me all about it," said Jake, responding to the excitement in his friend's voice, the kind of spontaneity which would probably frighten his mother.

"I've found one for you. Cheap as chips."

"What? What have you found?"

"A Beemer. It's a CAT-B. And only three-hundred notes."

"CAT-B?" Jake tried to recall the definitions of the four categories of vehicle write-off he'd recently read about online. "Does that mean it's roadworthy?"

"A BMW? For three-hundred? Roadworthy? You having a laugh?"

When Harry lapsed into caustic laughter, Jake tried hard to salvage some identity from his faux pas. "Yeah, sorry. I got confused. I've just been, er, playing GTA on the PC. Head's all over."

"CAT-B," said Harry, with all the expertise of the son of a mechanic, "means that the vehicle has to be salvaged for parts. But that doesn't mean we can't use it for what *we* want to use it for."

Jake's realisation of his mistake caused him to flinch, even though he knew that these issues didn't matter. He guessed such habits of thought were pressed deep inside him, almost woven into his DNA. But he was eager to overcome that kind of nonsense.

"You mean drag racing?" he asked, reflection on the computer games he hadn't actually played this evening reigniting his excitement.

"Draaaaaag," his friend replied. Then they arranged to meet tomorrow, after Jake had attended to more responsible issues, like his schooling.

Jake's dad had "never had the chance to go to university," as he often reminded him. But, despite having done well for himself since – he was the owner of a car repair garage and ran a fleet of taxis in town – he seemed keen for his son to aspire to academic heights.

Jake didn't mind too much – he had an aptitude for maths, and found that he could turn his hand to the core sciences too – but he guessed that the private school he'd attended since he was seven had restricted his development in more spontaneous ways, problematizing his enjoyment of stuff he felt drawn towards.

Cars were a case in point. Ever since he'd started playing driving simulators on consoles, he'd been thrilled by the prospect of one day owning a vehicle. In his early teens he'd pored over magazine articles and brochures, eyeing up Ferraris, Porsches and Bentleys. Despite his family's modest affluence, however, he knew that these brands were out of his range, certainly when just starting out in life. All the same, he held out hopes of owning a used German car – an Audi, a

Merc or even (the vehicle for which he'd developed a peculiar fetish, he didn't know why) a BMW.

When he reached Harry's house later that afternoon, he spotted the familiar ageing recovery truck parked in the short driveway. His friend's dad mustn't be working today, and this pleased Jake, because the man was always warm and welcoming – really tuned into youngsters – and that felt like something Jake lacked in life.

As soon as Harry responded to his knock at the peeling front door, he said, "Don't bother coming in. We're going straight back out. You got the money?"

Jake had stopped off at an ATM while walking from school to this slummy area of the small North Yorkshire town. He was just glad that he no longer had to wear a uniform; some of the lads who hung around on street corners hereabouts were unlikely to show much appreciation of that.

"Yeah, I got the money," he replied, fishing in one back pocket for the wad of notes (which, in any other circumstances, he'd have folded neatly in his wallet). "If I like what I see, I'll pay for it there and then."

Although Jake observed a trace of envy cross

his friend's face, he was pleased when it morphed into a bright smile. After all, Harry knew as well as Jake did that if they got hold of a decent off-road car, they'd do it up together and both be allowed to drive it.

Just then, Harry's dad emerged from the squat semi, dressed in his usual oily bib-and-braces. He had a racing cap perched on his short-cropped scalp.

"Lord, it's the boss's son come to check up on me," the man said, delivering a few playful shadow punches against Jake's wiry chest. He smiled, again showing Jake where his son got his happy-go-lucky demeanour from. There was only one envious lad here now.

"Let's go," said Harry, already darting towards the recovery truck.

"Do you want some money towards petrol, Mr Franks," Jake asked, walking alongside his friend's dad.

"No, that's okay, mate. It's only a few miles across town." Before he climbed into the driver's seat, he winked over the cab's roof. "Besides, I'm using the company's fuel. I don't suppose your dad will mind this particular errand on my day off, will he?"

Jake smiled but looked away, getting into the truck beside Harry. The truth was that Jake hadn't told his dad that he planned to buy a car, let alone a damaged one. It was his money – he'd saved it from his generous monthly allowances – but even so, at only seventeen years old, he reckoned he should have sought parental approval first, if only to avoid a shit load of hassle. Hell, he'd only got his licence a matter of months ago. Dad had made some vague promise about buying him a vehicle "if he did as well as expected" in his exams later this year, but that just felt like another example of his subtle methods of control.

The truck choked twice before breaking into a song, a real scotch-raddled bassline with an accompanying percussion of strained springs and loosening bolts. But eventually the vehicle got going, leaving behind a dark trail of smoke as it rattled into town, which, to Jake's relatively inexperienced mind, suggested... what? Bad head gasket? Failing pistons? Something to do with the cylinder head, anyway.

Then they'd reached the place selling the £300 car. After their brief telephone conversation last night Harry had sent Jake some photos of the vehicle by email, and it certainly looked okay. It was a 2003 coupé, dark blue and in pretty good condition. With less than 100,000 miles on the clock, Jake had begun to grow suspicious, but then he'd spotted the damage it had sustained: something big and heavy – another vehicle, presumably – had ploughed into its side, crumpling the driver's door and the rear quarter panel. Although the engine and transmission were seemingly unaffected, there might be unseen damage – hence the insurance company Category B write-off status.

"If you're just going to use it for drag racing, lads, a twisted chassis won't be much of an issue," said Harry's dad as the three of them alighted from the truck and started pacing across to the salvage yard's standalone cabin. "You'll get a few clunks and groans, and probably some irregular tyre wear, but as long as the thing goes, who gives a fuck, eh?"

Jake thought his mum might have collapsed if she'd just heard the man's coarse language, but Jake laughed along with his friend as they all stepped inside the yard's makeshift office.

A few minutes later they were outside again. The proprietor – a middle-aged man with either mischievous or dangerous wrinkles making his eyes spark – led them to the vehicle Harry's dad had called ahead about.

"Grabbed it at auction a few days ago. Only put it online yesterday. Ye gonna haff to be quick if you wanna take it off me hands, boys."

Jake briefly wondered whether it was possible to mangle more words in a single sentence, but then switched his attention to the BMW. From this angle - the undamaged side - it looked pristine, a real beauty. There was a ripple over the front wheel arch and some rust on the bottom panels, but these blemishes weren't as bad as he'd expect on a 14 year-old car. He loved it at once – that striking design like a big prowling cat – its panther-esque snout, its see-in-the-dark eyes and its ground-hugging body. Its engine, he knew, would purr, and the whole vehicle would create quite a buzz on the off-road racing circuit he and Harry often visited in countryside out of town.

"Okay, I'll ta—" he began, but got no further in making his non-negotiated offer when Harry's dad stopped him short.

Mr Franks had stepped around the far side of the car, presumably surveying the damage it had sustained. His face, ordinarily bright-eyed and cheerful, looked confused or even troubled. Jerking his head the way of the yard's owner, he said, "Do you know anything about how this car was written off?"

The other man, eyes still flashing in the wan October daylight, shrugged and lifted both hands. "I don't ask, mate. We're hardly talking big money here. Ye get what ya see at auctions."

"Sure, I know that." Mr Franks turned his attention back to the car. "It's just that this is...well, it's not like any write-off I've seen before."

Jake moved around to the other side of the BMW, following his friend's dad. At once he saw what he was getting at: close up, the crumpled door and rear quarter panel didn't look as if another vehicle had hit them at all. The damage was more diffuse, appearing to affect the whole side of the car. Anything else on the road would have gone in at knee-height, its front bumper causing a bulge. But this looked as if something less rigid had charged it – an animal, maybe, and one as big as a truck.

Jake shook his head, closing down stupid mental images of wild elephants or rhinos occupying the UK. Watching the two men eyeing one another warily, he said to the yard owner, "It's like you said, mister. We're hardly talking big money here. I'll give you £300 for it, just as your advert says."

He hadn't intended to shame his friend's dad – to him, such a figure probably *was* big money, even in full-time employment – but even though the man's face now looked concerned, Jake was determined to have what he'd come for.

Twenty minutes later, with the paperwork sorted out in the portacabin office, he found himself the owner of a real car.

~

There was trouble after they transported the BMW back to Jake's house on the outskirts of town. By now it was getting dark, the chill autumn air laden with drizzle. Jake's family home was set in its own grounds, with plenty of space at the head of its driveway for any number of cars. His mother's smart hatchback was there (perfect for shopping and all the busybody voluntary work she got involved with), and so was his dad's sensible Volvo estate. It was only 5pm, but once he'd done the rounds of his empire, Dad did a lot of work from home.

Harry's dad had just got the car off the back of the truck when the property's front door opened and Jake's dad thundered out, forehead corrugated with creases.

"Could someone kindly tell me what's going on?" he bellowed, perceiving at once who appeared to be responsible for this intrusion in his rarefied life: a man he employed, and using a company vehicle to perform the deed.

That was when Jake began to look sheepish, sneaking a glance at Harry's dad with apologetic eyes.

"Christ, you haven't told him, have you?" Mr Franks said, turning quickly to face his approaching boss. "Look, man, I didn't kn—"

"I'd sooner hear it from Jake, if that's all the same with you, Kevin. In fact, I'll deal with you later."

Harry responded most noticeably to this barked threat, staring at his dad in desperation, as if he knew how badly a loss of employment would affect his family. But then Mr Franks – Kevin – took a hold of his son and drew him away from the conflict about to get underway nearby.

"Come on, Harry, let's give Mr Hughes and Jake some time to sort this out."

They didn't need long. A noisy altercation soon struck up, with both taking predictably opposite positions. Jake defended his right, as a seventeen year-old with a driver's licence, to possess his own vehicle; his dad claimed that Jake wasn't an adult yet and still needed parental approval to do adult things, especially driving in "such a wreck." Jake defended the car and said that he wouldn't be using it on the streets anyway, citing the off-road tracks just out of town; his dad said that this was even worse, and asked him whether he'd considered his mother's feelings about this.

"You have your exams to concentrate on too," his dad went on, raising his voice only because there were no neighbours within earshot. "On top of that, you'll show the whole family up. Don't you care at all?"

"Yeah, but that's *all* you and Mum care about, Dad. Showing up the family. I'm not even doing anything wrong here!"

Dad turned to address the vehicle, which currently revealed its damaged side. "Just look at the *state* of this car. It's certainly not staying here."

"Yes, it is."

"No, it isn't."

"I own it, Dad. There's nothing you can do about that."

There was a silence, broken only by some animal prowling at a distance, presumably seeking quarry with surreptitious manoeuvres.

Jabbing a thumb over one shoulder, Jake's dad said, "Right, get inside the house now." He turned on Harry and his dad, who'd already climbed back inside the recovery truck. That was when he pointed at the driver. "I'll speak to you in the morning, Kevin. You mark my words I will."

"That isn't fair!" Jake heard his friend cry from inside the vehicle's cab. But then his dad silenced him, started up the truck – there were three attempts this time as it spluttered hoarsely on rough fuel – and finally backed away from the broad forecourt.

This left Jake, standing with his handful of paperwork and the BMW's keys, at the mercy of more parental tyranny. But he didn't give his dad another opportunity to put the rest of the world ahead of him. Jake turned to his car, unlocked it with the key fob, tugged open that buckled door, and then climbed inside. He stayed there until his dad eventually went back into the house, and a good deal longer, too.

The car wasn't roadworthy and couldn't be insured, but that hadn't got in the way of the fun Jake had already had with it. After attending dutifully to his schoolwork (he and his parents hadn't discussed compromises, just coexisted in tense silence for days), he'd driven the vehicle around their plot of land, performing handbrake turns and doughnuts once he'd got his confidence.

On the first weekend after the purchase Harry had cycled over and the two friends had spent some time figuring out how much of the Beemer could be realistically repaired. Harry said that Jake's dad had only sulked with his own at work lately, so Harry assumed that his old man's job was secure and that Harry had been worrying over nothing.

Jake had first met Harry at the garage about a year ago. After only a few minutes' awkward conversation, they'd realised that they shared an interest in computer games, and by the time they'd started swapping software they'd become fast friends.

Jake didn't have many close companions at his exclusive school (the only one in town); the lads there were heavy-going, already mindful of future career pathways and personal ambitions. Jake wasn't particularly focused on such matters; he simply wanted to have a bit of fun in life, something he felt had been denied him for a long time.

"I reckon we can beat out most of the crumples," Harry said, running a finger along the BMW's wounded flank. "But short of a new door, it's never going to look perfect, is it?"

"At least it locks and unlocks," Jake replied, but he was troubled by another matter at the moment, one he'd thrust aside every time it had occurred to him during the several days he'd owned the car. Drawing a sharp breath, he said, "What do you think caused this damage, mate?"

"Dunno. Maybe a truck. It had to be something big enough to hit the whole side."

"Yeah, but what could *that* be?" Jake paced forwards, joining his friend up close to the vehicle. "And have you seen *these*? They don't make any sense at all."

He was pointing at a series of savage tears just below the driver's window, as if someone had attacked the bodywork there with an axe. The sharp edges had rusted over, but even that wasn't as bad as further damage elsewhere, streaked down the single door on this side and also scudded across the BMW's roof. It looked as if the mad axeman had also flung acid at the vehicle.

"Maybe it was a stunt car used in Jurassic Park," Harry proposed unhelpfully, even though Jake appreciated his attempt to lighten the moment.

Before he was able to speculate further, Jake felt as if he was being observed and he glanced across at the woodland flanking his family's property. What had he expected to emerge from there – some savage beast with great ripping claws, spitting saliva as corrosive as battery acid? But that was when he realised the true location of his watcher: the house. With his dad away at work, his mother was spying on him from behind the lounge curtains.

"Come on, let's start cleaning this thing up," Jake said, recalling how much litter had been left inside the vehicle by its previous owner. He'd held back from tackling it all until his friend was here. "You work on the outside – try to get some of that weird stuff off the paintwork – while I sweep it out."

"Message received and understood, sah!" Harry snapped back, and Jake didn't care for the authority this appeared to grant him. If anything, he felt that Harry – worldly, relaxed, struggling to get by in life without losing his sense of fun – was by far the superior youngster.

As Harry scrubbed the bodywork with wire wool, Jake used a carrier bag to collect all the screwed up detritus in the front and rear foot-wells. Here were petrol receipts, food wrappers, a few squashed drink cans (worryingly, one alcoholic), and a newspaper dating back over a year. Whoever had once owned the car must have been a bit of a slob, even though that didn't fit with Jake's image of a typical BMW owner. Weren't the coupé models usually driven by youngish well-to-do males?

When Jake poked his hand blindly under the driver's seat, he chanced upon something hard and thin, only a few inches long and wide. It felt like plastic. He pulled it out at once, confirming his initial impression. It was an identity card, in this case that of the town's library, belonging to someone called Brian Portney.

Was this the original owner of the car? "Brian" didn't sound like the forename of any young buck, but at least his gender conformed to Jake's stereotypical understanding of Beemer owners. There was no photo of this guy, but his date of birth looked familiar, as it was close to Jake's dad's: November 1968.

Jake was about to climb out and show Harry what he'd found when a curious impulse stopped him. Instead he pocketed the library card, pretending he'd never chanced upon it. He swept the car's matted carpets, wondering what he planned to do later in the day, once his friend had returned home and Jake was alone in his bedroom.

~

Dinner that evening was a tense affair, Jake's dad continuing his campaign of sulks and Mum ably assisting with similar covert methods. The truth was that, short of threatening to throw him out of the house, they had no legal right to tell him to sell the BMW. So they'd all reached a tenuous impasse, the parents too stubbornly proud to back down while Jake felt bewildered and confused.

In comparison to that, the mystery of his car's previous owner and how the vehicle had been written-off seemed almost innocuous. Alone in his room, Jake typed Brian Portney's name into his favoured search engine. Once a page full of results appeared onscreen, he scrolled through them, dismissing most as irrelevant but then chancing upon one which looked promising, an article in the only local newspaper, dating back several months.

Once the link opened, he read about a tragic case in which a former schoolteacher – one Brian Portney, aged 52 – had been found battered to death in his town centre home. There was a blurred photo of the guy, looking grey, moustached, and rather anonymous. Portney had apparently lived alone, which had made police suspect that he was an easy target for burglars. Indeed, when a neighbour had alerted the authorities to the fact that his curtains hadn't been drawn back in days, investigators had found a number of possessions missing from his property, including a vehicle he usually left in his driveway.

That was all the online article mentioned – that a "car was missing." Jake returned to the newspaper's homepage and carried out a further search of its database. But no further information could be acquired. If the BMW had once belonged to poor old Brian Portney, Jake would have to seek confirmation elsewhere.

After switching back to the only article concerning this story, Jake made a note of the home address included in the text and then closed down his PC. He wasn't sure he'd sleep too well that night; a range of troublingly vague reflections occupied his skull, and he was uncertain about how easy it would be to get rid of them.

~

The following day was a study period but, following an unsettled night packed with odd dreams, Jake felt too wired to focus on revision. After a quick breakfast of toast and jam, he left the house, heading at once across town for the address he'd jotted down the previous evening.

It was a shame that he hadn't been able to drive here, but, despite what his mum and dad currently thought about him – the terrible embarrassment he'd caused the family – Jake wasn't a lawbreaker and had no desire to do wrong. Why would he ever need to? Short of unconditional love, he'd always had everything he wanted in life.

That couldn't be true of whichever miscreant had broken into Brian Portney's home. Jake wondered if this youth (at any rate, he assumed it was a youngster, and probably male, too) had been caught yet, and how the stolen car had sustained the damage it had. When he reached the property in question, which remained ghoulishly boarded up, he spotted a neighbour out in his own front yard, keeping a wary eye on Jake's activities.

This elderly man had every right to be cautious, especially if he suspected more trouble hereabouts. It might be a good time for Jake to have been wearing his posh school uniform, but that was a childish thought; he was very nearly an adult now and must take responsibility for himself.

He walked across to the man standing in front of his squat terraced home, greeting him with a hoisted hand and a smile, both social skills he realised he'd acquired from either

Harry or his friendly dad. At any rate, the act put the other at his ease, and by the time they got talking, Jake felt as if he could ask whatever he wished.

Once the guy had made all the usual enquiries Jake attracted from elders – how old was he? Did he have a girlfriend? Was he going to get some good qualifications? – Jake tackled head on the issue preoccupying him.

"I heard about a guy who lived around here once – I think he was called Brian Portney. Apparently he was killed in his home. Do you know anything about that?"

"We don't like talking about him," the old fella said, much to Jake's surprise given that Portney had been the victim of such a shocking crime.

"Why not?" Jake asked, sensing his heart rate step up, even though he couldn't think of any sensible reason why.

The neighbour scowled, adding a hundred more wrinkles to the thousands on his face. "He was up to no good, wasn't he? That's why they sacked him from the school. It was what they found on his computer."

What did the man mean – child

pornography? That was the go-to reason among middle-aged men to account for social ostracism, as well as prevention from working with youngsters. Jake recalled thinking last night that Portney's age – only 52 – was remarkably young for retirement. So was this what the guy's neighbour had meant?

Swallowing drily, Jake plucked up enough courage to broach the sensitive issue. But he didn't expect the response he received.

"No, not that. Christ, *that* might have been tame by comparison."

"Then what the hell do you mean?" asked Jake, growing so frustrated that he'd come very close to using a swearword in public.

The old man shook his balding head, hoisting a pointed finger heavenwards. "He was into all that occult nonsense, wasn't he? Black magic, pentagrams, spells and rituals. You name it, he'd had a dabble. That was why the newspaper went quiet about the whole business. What police found in his home once they'd raided it – dead animals were maybe the *least* horrible things – you wouldn't want to know about. Not if you want to sleep well at night, anyway. Not if you want to feel safe even during the daytime."

Although it was longer to get home this way, Jake took the country route back, hoping the quiet would help him think, allowing him to piece together all he'd learned into some coherent narrative.

He now owned a BMW with curious damage to one side, as if something other than another car had barged into it and delivered savage slashes to its bodywork, as well as corroding its paint. This vehicle had once belonged to a guy who'd been murdered by a burglar who'd presumably stolen the car along with other goods from the property. The man had also been interested in the Dark Arts, to such a degree that, if his aged neighbour could be believed, he'd lost his job.

Whatever did any of this mean? What had become of the person who'd broken into Portney's house and then made a getaway in his BMW? And was the damage the vehicle had suffered anything to do with this criminal's disappearance – from newspaper reports, if not in fact worse than that? From *life itself*?

Just then, Jake heard a sound up ahead. He

glanced that way at once, searching the overgrown fields to his left and right for signs of movement. He might have thought a cat lurked nearby, seeking mice on the soil underfoot; the presence of such a creature would certainly account for the subdued growling he thought he'd heard, as if a stealthy feline's manoeuvre was underway, with all accompanying sounds of hungry expectation.

But, the more he scrutinised the swaying grass, the less he believed that any animal occupied the territory around him. He continued walking at an accelerated pace, and it must have been the late-winter breeze sharp in his ears which now made him detect a buzzing sound. But that made no sense at all. Bees and wasps were summer creatures, flourishing in warm climates. Jake wasn't sure he'd ever seen either during the colder seasons, and besides, this noise – faint enough to imply distance – had seemed to belong to something much larger than that of any fingernail-sized insect.

It must have been a vehicle on a nearby street or even, Jake thought with cheering eagerness, off-road cars racing around a track. The place to which he planned to take his new vehicle was about half-a-mile from his current location, but with a strong wind in the right direction, maybe the sound could carry.

He didn't hesitate to dwell upon any of these suspicions, merely kept up his rapid pace until he'd reached his slumbering home. It was dark now, late afternoon, and the property's curtains twitched as he approached – just his mother looking out, determined to make him feel like the boy he no longer wanted to be.

~

"CAT-B" read the letter awaiting him in that day's post. It was from the DVLA and confirmed that, although the BMW could remain legally registered with an owner, it mustn't ever be driven on a public road.

Jake already knew this, but, in the context of everything he'd experienced lately, something about the communication troubled him. It bugged him all evening, blocking his capacity to memorise equations, learn chemical symbols, and absorb the counter-intuitive principles of quantum physics. By bedtime (his mum and dad had long since stopped wishing him goodnight, so that was one less thing to be troubled by), his mind was awash with squirming recollections, impressions and suspicions, to such a degree that at least one bad dream seemed inevitable.

So it proved. He imagined that he was taking the longer route home again, moonlight saturating his rural surroundings. That was when he heard that noise once more, a disquieting cross between a rampant feline's snarl and the sound of an angry wasp. When he glanced across at an overgrown field nearby, he noticed something parting the head-high grass at a distance, but coming quickly closer, closer and closer. That noise grew louder, an insane buzzing which cut the air all around like some atomic chainsaw. Only seconds later, the thing headed his way revealed itself, crushing aside a final row of obediently fey crop.

It was his own BMW, a coupé model and midnight blue. But this one was undamaged, and in the front seats sat two men. On the driver's side was Brian Portney, looking as grey and blurred as he had in the newspaper photo. Beside him, smiling with untypical glee, was Jake's dad.

That was when Jake awoke from the nightmare, bathed in a cold, discomforting sweat.

~

It was another few weeks before Jake and Harry were ready to take the car drag racing. By this time, they'd knocked out the dented door and panels to make them look presentable and resprayed the spliced bodywork, along with most of that missing paint. Harry's dad had helped with some aspects of the work, but as he was "still in the doghouse with the boss" (the man's typical playful way of referring to such occupational hassle), he hadn't wanted to push his luck at the town centre garage.

Two nights before they'd take the Beemer on a solo run around the off-road track, Jake visited Harry at home and had supper with his parents. This was a playful, chatty experience, and Harry's mum, probably as a consequence of limited household funds, had handmade a delicious pie far better than the premade supermarket stuff Jake's mother always bought.

"Did you ever find out anything about the previous owner of your new car, Jake?" asked Mr Franks, his voice audibly wary, as if he realised that he was referring to troubling material. Jake wasn't sure how the man had known Jake would be interested in the matter, but he supposed that was how parents in tune with youngsters worked.

At first Jake felt reluctant to reveal the knowledge he'd acquired, but then, as his dreams had settled back lately to reflect only his usual anxieties, he mentioned that dethroned schoolteacher Brain Portney.

The kitchen-serving-as-a-dining-room grew immediately silent.

Jake looked around, fearing he'd said or done the kind of thing which earned him similar disapproval from his parents – licked his knife in public, placed his elbows on the table, or left his cutlery unpaired on a plate once he'd finished a meal. But that was when Harry, after issuing a wet sneeze without covering his mouth, spoke up.

"Portney used to work at my school. He was a right weirdo. God knows why he chose a job with kids, 'cos he friggin' hated 'em."

With only a handful of schools in town, Jake wondered why he hadn't suspected that the guy had been employed where Harry received his education. Now he considered the matter, Portney's former home was only a minute's walk from that institution.

"What was he like, mate?" Jake asked, trying to adapt his phrasing to the easy-going vibe of this evening. "What did he teach you?"

"He was into all the sciences, wasn't he, Harry?" Mr Franks said, resurrecting the worried frown he'd worn the day Jake had bought his car. "I can't remember much more about what happened, to be honest. But I know he got the sack and the school was quite cagey about all that. They don't tell parents owt these days."

"He taught physics and chemistry," Harry added, but then suffered a bout of coughing which lasted nearly a minute. When he finally got his voice back, he said through a nose full of snot, "He kept going on about discipline, how kids these days had no discipline, and needed more than the State could ever do to control them. We all used to think he was just jealous because he lived alone and was old and scared and bitter about that."

Later that evening, after Jake had bid goodnight to Harry's pleasant mum, Mr Franks offered to give him a lift home. On this occasion the truck started on the fifth try ("Needs a new cam-belt urgently," he explained, "but I just haven't had time to work on it,"), and once it got rolling through the moonlit streets it threatened to stall several times.

Approaching Jake's house Mr Franks said, "I'm back here on Saturday to take you, Harry and the Beemer over to the racetrack out of town, aren't I?"

"If that's still okay, Mr Franks. I can give you some petrol money if you like."

The driver slowed the vehicle on the house's driveway, glancing cautiously across at the property. The curtains in the lounge had just twitched, suggesting that Jake's parents had expected him home earlier. Jake was only surprised that neither had called him on his mobile, as if he was still a child.

"No, seriously, it's fine, son," Harry's dad said, keeping the truck idling noisily, presumably to prevent its engine from cutting out. "You're doing all this for my lad, too, so really, it's cool."

Jake suddenly felt all warm inside; just then, he didn't want to get out of the cab and deal with the inquisition he'd inevitably face after entering his home. Although he'd attended to all his revision before setting out earlier today, that issue was only ever a front for more sinister forms of control.

"Bye, then." Jake popped open the truck's door.

"Stay strong," the driver said, clenching a fist and raising it, as if he knew, having worked for the man for years, how difficult Jake's father could be. "Oh, and enough of the Mr Franks nonsense – it's Kevin, okay?"

"Okay. Thanks, Kevin," Jake said, and quickly fled the truck with something approaching tears, which even the sight of his semi-restored Beemer did little to combat. The sad truth was that he'd wanted to call the departing guy "Dad."

~

That night he suffered another bad dream in which the territory all around him – parts of his home, many country fields, a section of the off-road track – felt pregnant with menace. All he heard, however, was a whisper, delivered forcefully from a moody sky. "*CAT-B...CAT-B...CAT-B*," it said, the voice resembling that of an animal or a particularly noisy insect. "*CAT-B...CAT-B...CAT-B...*"

~

On the day of the big event, Jake's lift arrived right on time. But he was surprised to see only his friend's dad sitting in the cab upfront.

"Harry's streaming with a cold," Mr Franks – Kevin – explained after climbing out of his truck. "He's lost his voice and basically feels like death warmed up. He sends his apologies and says he'll make it next weekend for sure. But he knew how much you were looking forward to this and insisted I come along anyway."

Jake's initial response was private panic – he'd have to go to the track alone and meet many other rough youngsters – but then he realised that he might be comfortable in such company; it could help him to be more like the person he felt inside, which his schooling had tried hard, and yet failed, to overrule.

"Sorry to hear that, Mr Fr—I mean, Kevin. But will you still pick me up when I'm finished? I won't be able to drive home in my car, will I?"

"Of course I wi—" Kevin started to reply, but got no further because that was when Jake's dad appeared, skulking from the house like some clumsy predator.

"Is that *my* petrol you're running in that truck, Kev?" he asked, his voice actually good-natured, as if this – the kind of acerbic joke Jake had often observed working men exchange – was the closest he came to affection. "Only joshing, mate. Glad you could help out."

Perhaps after a lengthy "cold war" period, Jake's dad had decided to relent; maybe seeing his only child interacting with another man had served as a wakeup call. Whatever the truth was, Jake remained wary of his dad's newfound enthusiasm for his interest in drag racing. After all, it wasn't as if he'd been welshing on his schoolwork; both his parents had observed him swotting on a daily basis and he hadn't missed a single lesson in the classroom. Dad must have another motivation for revising his attitude on the matter.

"I'll bring him home at a reasonable hour, Mr Hughes," Kevin said, and despite all the years he'd worked for the family's garage, Jake realised that his dad must never have given Kevin permission to address him by his first name.

"Ten o'clock, I'm thinking. That seem fair to you, Jake?"

It was the time he'd previously agreed with Kevin, so he issued a quick, compliant nod.

Dad's presence while Kevin loaded the Beemer onto the back of his truck felt like that of some meddlesome insect; a sub-audibly threatening buzz in the background. But soon the car was ready to depart and so, with relief, was Jake.

"Don't do anything to upset your mother," Dad called in another semi-comic, semi-serious voice. Then, as the chugging truck pulled out of the driveway, Jake spotted another brief twitch of curtain at the front of the house.

One day, he thought as the truck accelerated mercifully on, *I'd like to have all those fucking windows boarded up like they were at Brian Portney's place.*

~

The event, as it turned out, was terrific fun and everyone was very welcoming. Once Harry's dad had left him alone with an encouraging wink, Jake had been the centre of attention for a while, his Beemer cutting a fine (if slightly crumpled) figure among a number of midrange hatchbacks and souped-up saloons. The other lads there, most in their 20s and a few as young as him, were bullish in demeanour and free with their language, but, as Jake had spent so much time with Harry over the last year, he found himself fitting in well, swearing and laughing with natural ease.

When he finally climbed inside the BMW, ready to make his practised moves, he wondered whether his parents, both middleclass aspirants on the strength of the business's earnings and a terror of social embarrassment, weren't just pretenders, secretly fearing that spontaneous behaviour would expose who they truly were. Deep down, Jake might also suffer the same crude thoughts and feelings, his upmarket schooling little more than a tenuous facade. In fact, could Jake-in-the-eyes-of-his-parents be who his mum and dad privately wished themselves to be?

The insight was pitiable, but Jake refused to let it get in the way of who he thought he was becoming. That was when he trod on the Beemer's accelerator pedal, making the engine roar like a beast.

Leave discipline to those who fear themselves, he reflected, putting the car into gear; *and let me embrace who I really am.*

He let rip.

Jake spent several hours tearing around the track, racing other vehicles, drifting around corners, and performing stunts like handbrake turns and doughnuts, all of which he'd rehearsed at home lately. He enjoyed every minute, and as dark descended to leave only the moon to illuminate nearby fields, he realised that he didn't want to leave. His nose was packed with the scent of scorched rubber, his eyes and ears smarting with kicked up dirt. But it felt wonderful; he simply wanted it to go on and on.

After nine pm, however, most of the other drivers started leaving. Some had clearly bought write-offs like his, loading them back onto trucks they or friends also owned; others had snapped up cheap roadworthy cars, departing the track via a narrow country lane. But, as Jake watched headlamps splash away amid endless trees and overgrown grass, there was no sign of his lift, of Kevin Franks arriving in that ageing recovery vehicle.

Ten o'clock came and went, and then five-past, ten-past, quarter-past. By now, all but a handful of his fellow drag racers had fled. One guy tapped something under his bonnet to summon a reluctant spark from its engine; at last he got it going, departing with several of the other dalliers, all honking horns and flicking abrasively comic V-signs at Jake through their windscreens. Jake reciprocated with a forced smile, but then, all alone in the dark, he wondered whether he'd made his first big mistake in life.

Maybe his parents had been right to worry and to hassle him so much; perhaps the world *was* a dangerous place. From the dark Jake heard something out on the prowl, presumably a nocturnal animal, seeking seasonal sustenance. But he refused to continue thinking like that; he was an adult now and shouldn't capitulate to foolish fears.

He plucked out his mobile, scrolling through the list of numbers stored in its memory. Should he call his dad, giving him (not to mention Jake's mum) the satisfaction of proving his son wrong? He blanched at the prospect, but what other option did he have? Harry's dad, Kevin Franks, had let him down, probably even forgetting that Jake was here. That was what other people were like. This was something else he'd have to get used to as he tugged himself free of an overprotective childhood.

Jake was about to despair, even holding back childish tears, when his phone rang. He glanced at the screen: it was Harry calling. Thank God. Jake answered at once.

But it wasn't his friend, after all.

"Jake? So sorry, son. It's Kevin here. I've just managed to get your number. I had to use Harry's phone. He's asleep in bed, so it took me a while to find it. Anyway, I've got a big problem. The truck won't start. I reckon the cam-belt's finally given up the ghost. Honestly, the thing won't budge an inch.

"Now listen, have you got some money on you? Can you call for a taxi? Either that or walk along that lane to the A-road – you can get a bus back. The last one passes at eleven. Just leave the car there – I'll collect it tomorrow evening, using another vehicle from the garage. I'll come to your place and pick you up first, of course.

"Look, man, I'm sorry again. I shoulda seen this coming. I just haven't had the time to work on the truck amid all the jobs coming in lately at the garage."

So Jake's dad was responsible for this problem, too.

But Jake thrust away these borderline paranoiac and rather precious thoughts in favour of finding a suitable solution to his dilemma. He was so relieved that Kevin hadn't let him down that he forgave the man at once.

"Thanks for calling and letting me know," he said, struggling to hold his voice steady. "Please don't worry about me. I'll get home safely somehow."

Moments later, Jake hung up, wondering exactly how he'd achieve this. Yes, he had a few notes in his wallet, but he was loath to use the money for a taxi, which would likely cost at least a fiver. He could buy more petrol for next weekend's drag meeting with such a sum.

A bus ride was a better option, but was it worth hanging around (Jake checked his mobile screen: it was ten-thirty) another half-an-hour to make the relatively short ride back into town? He realised that it was only a couple of miles to his house; he could walk it in less than an hour.

But why take that option when he had a mode of transport right here: the Beemer in perfect working order.

The thought felt dangerous but he entertained it all the same. He didn't want to leave the car here. What if vandals found it and decided to trash it, leaving a burnt-out husk near the track? He knew it wouldn't take long to drive home. What were the chances of police being about on a quiet night like this anyway? The town was hardly a hotbed of crime at the worst of times, and Jake thought it unlikely that he'd get pulled over during the ten minute ride.

The real issue, however, was what his parents would say. But should that really concern him anymore? If he didn't get caught, nobody need ever know; he wouldn't bring shame on the family. Like so much else between them – the covert tyranny his mum and dad had brought to his life for as long as he could remember – this could be their little secret, even a little revenge on Jake's part, a firm reminder that, after all the stubborn resistance he'd shown lately concerning his car, *he* now had power, too.

He was an adult, capable of making independent decisions. Yes, this one was questionable, but what was the alternative? A return to being manipulated, to conforming with dismaying complicity, to feeling dead, dead, dead.

Feeling more alive than he had in years, Jake climbed back inside his vehicle and gunned its sweetly purring engine.

~

The thing struck him halfway along the country lane. It came from his left, through a field full of grass as tall as his car. At first he perceived nothing more than a blur as a considerable bulk slammed against the BMW, surely causing as much damage to the passenger side as had once been delivered to the driver's door. The whole vehicle rocked on its springed haunches, creaking and groaning in the wake of such a heavy-bodied assault. Was this savage attacker some other type of transport – bigger, stronger, faster?

None of it made sense. Jake, reeling with confusion and incipient panic, tried hard to keep the Beemer on the narrow kerbless lane. The thing - now in his rear-view mirror, having gathered its strength for a second sortie - promptly scuttled forwards.

In what little moonlight fell behind his car, Jake spotted angular, segmented joints like those of an insect's limbs, each terminating in great ripping claws more becoming of a giant cat. The thing's head was also feline in structure, though what tiger or lion had ever boasted such rigid stingers protruding from its scalp, let alone a lengthy proboscis brandishing a suckered snout?

Jake found that the shocking sight of the thing in his wake had caused him to lighten up on the accelerator. But when it came at him again, making a terrible buzzing which filled the air all around with an almost radioactive atmosphere, he switched his attention back to the car, thrashing its engine and yet still failing to overrule the approaching sound of whatever hideous entity followed.

For a moment, in his fear, Jake thought he'd accidentally nudged on the car's stereo, locating only frantic static and distorted human voices. But then the frightful cacophony above the sound of his racing vehicle was silenced altogether as the thing struck home once more, this time inflicting similar bulges and tears in the vehicle's rear as those mighty claws augmented the damage already affected by that bulky body.

CAT-B, thought Jake in mounting delirium. *This is Brian Portney's demented supernatural disciplinarian.*

Cat-bee.

These thoughts flitted through his mind like a knife through flesh, but as the buzzing, hissing, scrabbling combatant clambered upon the moving car's roof, nothing else would come to him, even though somewhere amid such mental chaos his dad's face was visible, along with that of his mum.

The thing's razor-sharp claws penetrated the top of his beloved Beemer, threatening to open it up like a tin can, perhaps the way it had once disposed of a murderous burglar. Jake slammed on the brakes. He'd been travelling at nearly 60 miles per hour, but the suddenness of the action caused the creature to topple awkwardly forwards, crashing onto the bonnet and then collapsing in a heap several yards in front of the radiator grill as the car came to a halt, its nose dipping as if in fear.

For long seconds Jake saw nothing more than the thing's mottled hide, covered in tiny erect hairs like that of some magnified wasp, but then it began to reorient itself, rising up from patchy tarmac, like a wild cat about to retaliate.

Seconds later, it started making its noise again, that fretfully rasping buzz, sounding like some petrol-thirsty chainsaw. The world around Jake – trees standing tower-like nearby, grass swaying in a tetchy wind, the moon somehow remaining stable in a sin-black sky – thrummed along with the thing's activity, its rapidly mounting menace.

It was only now that Jake realised that his car had stalled. Glancing frantically down, he twisted the key, trying desperately to spark the engine into renewed life. In his peripheral vision, that thing rose ever more, jagged limbs jerking into the posture of something eager to attack. Jake's vehicle choked and spluttered a few times, much like Kevin Franks' truck always had, but that was when the ignition held, making the engine roar once more.

Jake tramped anew on the accelerator, sending the BMW forwards at a hungry dash. It hit the creature forcefully until even its considerable mass – large as a lion, forceful as a bee – conceded to the car's momentum and was crushed beneath its wheels as Jake hurtled away, refusing to let up his speed.

He screamed. He cried unrestrained tears. And when he reached the B-road way beyond the stretch of unoccupied countryside, he finally halted his vehicle, climbed out, and started running along the kerbside.

He didn't stop until he'd reached home. After entering, he thrust aside the questions of his concerned parents and then shut himself in his room. He kept listening for sounds from outside, but all he heard was a wind rushing at his window, making it rattle in its frame. He didn't dare draw back his curtains; couldn't face looking out into the dark.

It was hours later, once his body stopped shaking and the terror of his encounter had induced exhaustion, that he got to sleep. His dreams were a montage of unspeakable visions, most of which he failed, or was too scared, to recall upon waking.

Later the following day, Kevin Franks turned up in his truck, just as he'd promised. Jake told his mum to let the man know that he didn't feel well and wouldn't be able to help pick up the BMW. He'd also given her the car's keys to pass along. Just then, Jake loved his mum and appreciated the fact that she was willing to help out, leaving him safe in the house. When his dad got home from work an hour later, Jake felt even more secure at home.

He knew that he wouldn't break the law a second time; he'd learned his lesson well. He doubted he'd call Harry for a while, if ever again. Jake also believed that he could live without the once appealing Kevin, who, despite making amends today, had disappointed him the night before. That simply wasn't good enough.

This was life, after all. You needed to be responsible. You needed to be disciplined.

When the mechanic turned up that evening with the battered hulk of Jake's Beemer on the back of his truck, Jake's dad went out to tell his employee (at his son's instruction) to take the vehicle to the nearest salvage yard. Vandals had obviously located the car and trashed it overnight. There couldn't have been anything else near the BMW – no mashed-up remains of some large unidentifiable creature – because Kevin never mentioned it. And this was what most concerned Jake. Perhaps he hadn't killed that thing after all.

CAT-B, he thought with an involuntary shudder, and wondered how badly his life had now been written-off.

~1~

"Where are you going?"

"Out."

"I can see that, mate. I hoped you could be more specific."

"Just…out, that's all," said Duncan, and Kenny realised that was all he'd get from his stepson.

Once the boy had exited the house and slammed the door, Kenny recalled that Duncan was sixteen now and could do as he pleased. All the same, after five years of living with him and his mother, Kenny had begun feeling protective. It hadn't been easy, what with Linda's medical condition, but time brought together people who, in other circumstances, might have little in common.

After boiling the kettle and making coffee, Kenny went upstairs. His lover had had another bad day, a migraine leading to nausea, and the master bedroom was in darkness, the curtains closed against countryside. Relocating to the Yorkshire Dales had been Kenny's attempt to give Linda and her son a better life than the Leeds council estate on which they'd previously resided. When the opportunity had arisen to switch his job to the small town of Skipton, Kenny had taken action. It had been a good move, even though the boy seemed to little appreciate it, while his mother had yet to show any recovery from the condition which had ailed her for years.

Kenny placed a mug of coffee on the bedside table and stooped over his sleeping lover, pushing dark hair from her face. It was her health difficulties which had led to them meeting, when he'd visited her home to assess her welfare needs. Duncan had been thirteen at the time, and with no father around, there'd been concern about his well-being. Linda had pleaded with Kenny not to take the boy into care, and Kenny had decided this was unnecessary. Her gratitude had surely resulted in their relationship.

He watched her rouse from sleep. She was beautiful, and he often asked himself why she'd agreed to spend her life with him. Kenny had had no serious relationship until his late teens and had come to Linda, at twenty-three, a virgin. An overprotected upbringing, involving a tearful mother and a spineless father, had left him withdrawn and yet sympathetic to people with difficulties. This had steered his choice of profession as well as resulting in a weakness for the likes of Linda and her difficult yet likeable boy.

Linda stirred in bed. Then, after opening her eyes, she said, "Oh hi. You're back from work. What time is it?"

He smiled at her gentle voice, which matched the strain fading from her eyes to a heart-warming tee.

"Just gone seven," he said, handing across the mug.

"Have you eaten already?" Linda quickly accepted the coffee and took a quick swallow. Before he could reply, she added, "And how about Dunc'?"

Kenny didn't feel jealous as she switched her attention to her son. He'd got over any such nonsense early in the relationship; he'd had to grow up fast.

"Yes, he and I had beans on toast together." He smiled mischievously. "He even grunted once. It was incomprehensible, but I nonetheless considered it an attempt at communication."

Linda laughed, revealing perfect white teeth. She was thirty-nine and looked ten years younger – in truth, little older than he was. She yawned, rubbing both eyes in turn with her free hand.

"I'm tired," she said, just as she often had during the last few years, after visiting a doctor to deal with a perpetual exhaustion that had problematised her life. Back in Leeds she'd neglected domestic responsibilities, and a part-time job in the high street had been blighted by frequent absences. She no longer needed to work, of course, but this hadn't made life much easier, for her or for Kenny.

She spoke again. "Where *is* Duncan anyway?"

"A good question, that," Kenny replied, typically using humour to marshal his unease. "I put the same one to him only ten minutes ago. And I was told, with frankly dazzling eloquence, that he was *going out*."

"Out?" Linda laughed again, but despite her amusement, she spoke more firmly. "Out where?"

"Rather difficult to say, my dear." He suddenly stood and walked around the bed, rising to his playful theme. "I first considered the theatre, but then thought better of that. After all, they're doing King Lear at the moment, and I know Dunc's favourite play is Hamlet."

Linda laughed again. She knew as well as he did that her son was more likely to be found killing aliens on X-Box than toiling over homework. All the same, realising Kenny's comments were affectionate, she remained amused.

Kenny was pleased about that. Despite having read all the medical literature, he still didn't fully understand M.E. He just felt that a playful attitude to life was likely to help. Linda had experienced a difficult past, and Kenny was sure drugs had been involved. What she needed now was someone to remind her that life needn't be cruel. He only had to reflect on his own past to realise how true this was, how he'd transitioned from ugly playground duckling to the lover of such a graceful swan.

As Kenny developed his joke further, he

observed his partner – serene face, sharp shoulders, soft arms – float across the surface of life, while underneath, unseen and frantic, she kicked like crazy.

"...I considered ballet classes...a fine arts course...voluntary work at a charity organisation..." he continued. In fairness, he didn't know about Duncan's problem, not back then – not when he still had so many things to learn about himself.

~2~

Kenny began to suspect that something was wrong when his stepson returned home that evening, long after nine o'clock.

Linda had gone back to sleep after a meal, and Kenny was watching a Champions League game on TV. After Duncan entered, he must have heard the crowd's roar, because instead of going straight up to bed, he came into the lounge, dropped into the armchair opposite the couch occupied by Kenny, and started talking.

Duncan communicating at all surprised Kenny, but the humour in his voice was even more suspicious. It was untrue to say that he'd struggled with the boy; with no biological father around (Linda hadn't talked much about him and Kenny hadn't asked), Duncan had accepted Kenny as his stepdad with little more than an indifferent smile. All the same, the boy's lack of openness often confused Kenny; he never knew whether he was saying the right things.

Wide eyes fixed on the TV screen, Duncan said, "That was *never* offside!" And moments later, "If they win, they're into the knock-out round, aren't they?" Then, "They need someone to drive them forwards in midfield, cos they've not been the same since Smithy left."

Kenny tried to respond enthusiastically, despite feeling wary. Early experiences in life had left him this way, suspicious of pretty much everyone around him. Just then, lapsing into a mindset he adopted daily at work, Kenny suffered a terrible thought.

Was Duncan taking *drugs*?

When the full-time whistle blew, Kenny reached for the remote control, turned down the volume, and then looked directly into the boy's eyes. "So, did you have a good time this evening?"

"Huh?"

Ah, the grunts return, thought Kenny, but was now determined to pursue his enquiry. "I was just wondering where you've been. You were gone for over four hours. Did you have fun?"

Duncan's eyes looked brighter than usual, but in the low light of the lounge Kenny struggled to detect any pupil dilation. When the boy glanced away, his voice reassumed its usual sullenness. "It was all right, I suppose." Then he got up promptly from the chair. "I'm off to bed now."

"Fair enough," Kenny replied, but then drew on a trick he often used in his job, as a way of getting offenders to betray themselves. "But I don't know how you'll sleep with your head buzzing like *that*."

With one foot already on the staircase up, Duncan hesitated, glancing briefly at Kenny with perhaps a touch of resentment in his expression. "What do you...mean?"

Kenny hesitated a moment but then smiled, pointing to the TV, on which a trio of pundits offered their post-match analysis. "After the game, mate. Two-nil to our lot, wasn't it?"

"Oh...yeah. Right. I get you."

Duncan turned away, and as he began

thumping upstairs, Kenny wondered whether he'd actually seen a look of relief just cross the boy's face.

~3~

It didn't have to be drugs. It might be a girl he'd met. That would account just as well for the boy's moody behaviour.

This possibility helped Kenny get through another long day at the office. Following recent government budget cuts, he'd been forced to become more stringent while reviewing welfare support applications, even though this went against his sympathetic nature. Many poorly understood conditions existed – Linda's M.E., for instance – but lately the council had limited his capacity to make discretionary judgements. It was sadly more than his job was worth to question these new, ironclad rules.

By the end of the day, Kenny had gained some perspective on his stepson's behaviour. Maybe Duncan had actually made new friends and realised that the move from Leeds was a good one. He might be too embarrassed to tell the man who'd brought it about how grateful he was.

While driving home, Kenny reflected on the feelings of safety he'd always enjoyed in Skipton. He'd grown up in a decent, if far from thriving, part of Bradford. Even there there'd been trouble, bullying and vandalism a particular problem. Gangs had loitered on street corners, drinking alcohol and intimidating passers-by. This had been back in the 1990s, when families had begun fragmenting and yoof culture had been on the rise. It had all grown worse since.

There was little of that here. Before selling his property in Leeds, Kenny had carefully considered the ideal place to live. He'd visited most of his favourite locations during childhood: Whitby on the northeast coast, the Scottish Borders, a few quiet towns in north Wales. But Skipton had been high on his list and was the only desirable place in which he could find a suitable job.

He took a longer route home, as he often did. He liked to park in a layby overlooking the countryside. He wished his parents had lived long enough to see how well he'd done for himself. An only child, Kenny had felt pressure to achieve something in life and only recently realised that this had much to do with his parents' need for status among peers. That had been especially true of his dad, a printing engineer who'd been obsessed by social mobility. Kenny had always felt an inner need to impress his father, even after the older man had died of cancer five years ago.

Was he finally beginning to overrule this treacherous part of himself? He looked again at the Yorkshire Dales – at waving trees, swaying grass, solid rocks – and realised that he probably was. Then he drove home.

~4~

Duncan failed to return home from school that evening.

Kenny had prepared the boy's meal after getting in from work. Linda had been in bed again, suffering an attack of vertigo, and Kenny had spent the evening downstairs, watching the national news, and then a documentary about unregulated foster homes, and finally a film starring some fading Hollywood superstar.

By eight o'clock, he'd begun to be concerned.

The boy had been late in the past, often after visiting a mate's house to play Xbox or the local park for a game of football. But on those occasions, he'd let Kenny or his mum know where he was. Although he was still interested in computer games and sport, he'd surely now, a bit older, be getting intrigued by other things, such as girls, booze and...

Kenny pushed aside these thoughts, unwilling to fret about the same things he had the previous evening. He was tired from work and knew that this was never a good time to consider important issues. He needed to think clearly, keep a level head. So what should he do next?

He was reluctant to trouble Linda. He also imagined what short shrift the police would offer if he called to report a sixteen year-old missing for only a few hours. Kenny advanced to the kitchen window and glanced outside. Although the street was deserted, it wasn't yet even dark. There was no need to worry; he should just settle back and watch the lousy film. When Duncan eventually returned, maybe Kenny could establish a few ground rules.

Once nine o'clock had come and gone,

however, he'd grown deeply concerned. He'd checked on Linda several times this evening and found her asleep. Perhaps he should wake her and share his concerns, even though this might complicate a vulnerable spell she was presently suffering. Reluctant to do that, Kenny reassured himself that there was still time for Duncan to show up yet, that it wasn't particularly late. But less than ten minutes later, he snatched up the landline telephone and prepared to dial. He'd just entered the first three digits of his stepson's mobile number when he heard the front door open.

After entering the kitchen at a hurry, Kenny saw Duncan standing next to the dining table. Kenny thought he was smiling, but as soon as Duncan glanced his way, his lips straightened and then he hoisted his school bag, like strangling a dog on a leash.

"I'm going to bed," he said, heading towards Kenny on his way to the staircase.

"Not so fast," Kenny replied, raising a hand to stop the boy's progress. They stood in that position for several seconds, struggling to adjust to a new phase in their relationship: physical contact. Kenny had often verbally disciplined the boy about trivial matters, but they'd never come to blows. Duncan had simply conformed to authority decreed by Kenny's superior age, and Kenny was thankful for that. He always felt uncomfortable exercising power. His late father had never found it easy to be strict, and Kenny supposed that such dispositions were either inherited or acquired.

Glancing down at Kenny's restraining hand, Duncan said, "Get off me. You're not..." The boy hesitated, as if conscious of the implications of his next words. But then he finished anyway: "...you're not my *dad*."

The comment stung Kenny, and for long seconds he felt out of mental focus. But after glancing elsewhere, at aspects of the house he worked hard to pay for, he realised that he deserved respect for other reasons.

"I *know* that, mate," he said with a conciliatory tone. "But how about you showing some decency, eh? You didn't come home from school and we were worried about you." Backing off a little, he tried deepening what little bond had already developed between them. "Look, I haven't told your mum about this. She's not well right now. You understand that, don't you? So why make things more difficult?"

"*I'm* not making things difficult," the boy said, face suddenly twisting up. "I mean, if I'm not here, how can I do anything wrong?"

"But *that's* the problem, isn't it?"

"Why? Why is it a problem?"

Kenny now stood face-to-face with the boy. Despite his out-of-character behaviour, Duncan appeared far from intoxicated. He'd never been cheerful, but his change in attitude was troubling. Kenny felt that he must get to its root before it affected Linda, which would unsettle the whole household. He'd seen this happen so often in his job and knew that only addressing problems at the earliest stage could prevent it.

"All we want to know is where you go each evening," said Kenny, keeping his voice as calm as possible. "We don't want to stop you visiting the place – well, not necessarily. We just need to know that you're safe."

"I'm safe. Believe me. I'm safer there than I could be elsewhere."

Kenny suddenly felt even more uneasy. "Safer than here, with your mum and..."

"*Much* safer than here."

"So...where do you go?"

The boy offered no immediate reply, just stepped backwards so that Kenny's hand fell from his chest. Moments later, his smile resurfacing, he started retreating upstairs and then said with trailing triumph: "I go to my dad's. My *real* dad's."

~5~

After Linda awoke from another long nap, Kenny wasted no time in addressing his concerns.

"We need to talk," he said, handing her a cup of tea. He'd just checked that Duncan was asleep in bed and had then entered the master bedroom and closed the door.

"That sounds ominous." Linda took the tea, scrabbled on the bedside table for pills – vitamin supplements and painkillers – and quickly swallowed a handful. Then she looked at him. "What is it, Kenny? Problems at work?"

He hesitated, trying to prevent his racing heart from compromising his voice. "Who was Duncan's father, Linda?" he asked.

Linda moved the cup from her mouth, as if she'd suddenly rather have access to alcohol.

Moments later, she gazed at him, looking angry and edgy. "You don't need to know that, Kenny. So let's just pretend you never asked."

"Linda, I'm afraid I do. It's Duncan, you see. He's—"

"'Dunc' is *exactly* why I won't talk about that...*man*." Her face was now full of pain. "He never wanted anything to do with him when he was born. Christ, he even *denied* being his father. He's a bad lot, Kenny. A waste of time."

"But..."

"I'm warning you. If you continue, you'll...you'll only make me sicker."

It had previously crossed Kenny's mind that occasionally some of his girlfriend's illness might be play-acting. This kind of suspicion arose from the nature of his work, an occupational hazard when dealing with welfare support claimants. Deep down, however, he knew that Linda's case was genuine. Whatever M.E. was, its symptoms could be devastating, and Kenny certainly had no wish to aggravate her condition. But at the same time, he was worried that Duncan's behaviour might lead to a shock from which she'd never recover. For this reason alone, he needed to tackle the problem immediately, even though doing so meant that he must know where Duncan went each evening: he had to know who the boy's father was. With a name, Kenny could identify a residential address on the electoral register. The only alternative – covertly following the boy after school – involved dishonesty, and Kenny was unwilling to resort to that.

Once Linda looked a little less uppity, he told her everything he'd recently suspected about Duncan and then what the boy had said earlier that evening. When he reached the most fractious part – "I go to my dad's. My *real* dad's," – he noticed Linda's facial expression shift from rage to sorrow.

"If that *bastard* has made contact after all this time..." She floundered, tears running down her cheeks. "He was a *drug addict*, Kenny. The truth is that everyone in the group I used to hang out with used the gear, including me. But God, *he* caned it every day. He wasn't capable of getting it up half the time, and was completely uninterested in doing so the other half. He was a *bad* lot, Kenny – a *very* bad lot."

Kenny had just sat on the bed to comfort her. He'd always been good at supporting others, while few, at least since his parents had died, had ever done the same for him. He'd felt embarrassed by Linda's sudden candid admissions about her previous life, but realised that his sheltered upbringing accounted for that. All the same, he hadn't been particularly surprised by his lover's revelations.

Releasing her from their embrace, he said, "Look, Linda, let me deal with this. But I'll need a name. I have no idea where Duncan goes at night. If you tell me where that might be, I can do something about it." He hesitated, weighing up what he planned to add, and then decided that in the circumstances duplicity was justifiable. "I have contacts in social services. I can find things out. So please, Linda, for the sake of Duncan, give me the guy's name."

Moments later, heavy medication perhaps rendering her compliant, she told him what he needed to know.

~6~

After reaching his office the following day, Kenny called his stepson's school to make sure the boy had turned up for classes. He had, but Kenny was also told that although Duncan had settled in well since moving into the area, concerns had been raised about his recent academic performance. Kenny said he'd make an appointment to discuss the matter with the boy's tutor, and then rang off.

Next, he accessed the electoral register. The surname his girlfriend had given him was unusual – *Paternak* – and coupled with the Christian name *Vincent*, Kenny thought it should be easy to trace the man. Thus it proved. Linda had said that Vincent Paternak had once lived in the north of Leeds, and that was where he still resided, in a semi that, other records revealed, he'd purchased from the council ten years earlier.

After telling colleagues that he had a meeting, Kenny left the office and didn't cease driving until he'd reached his destination. He parked at the end of the unkempt street, trying to figure out how long the same journey would take by public transport, surely the way Duncan travelled here each evening. It had taken Kenny an hour to arrive by car, and a bus trip would take twice as long. But that didn't make sense. If Duncan came after school, he wouldn't arrive until five-thirty and he was always back in Skipton by nine. That gave him and his biological father only ninety minutes together. What could they do in so little time? It was possible that the guy drove north to see the boy, but from social security records, Kenny had learned that Vincent Paternak hadn't worked in five years, which reduced the likelihood of him owning a reliable car.

After approaching the man's property, Kenny paced up its broken path. The house looked nigh on uninhabitable, all dirty brickwork and greasy windows. Kenny knocked on the door and awaited a response. Turning briefly to observe the street, he thought he saw a whitish figure dodge out of sight beyond a hedge along the pavement, but when he looked more carefully, nothing was there.

That was when the house's front door creaked open, and a short man, rake-thin and lacking a full set of teeth, put his head around the frame.

"You here about the council tax?" he said, with surprising deference given his roguish appearance. "Our Alice phoned yez last week – to explain the situation, like. We're getting it all together now. She's taken on extra shifts and that."

"Mr. Paternak?" Kenny spoke in a neutral voice, neither authoritative nor submissive. "Are you Vincent Paternak?"

"Could be." Suddenly the homeowner looked more evasive. "It might help if I knew who was asking, like."

"Mr. Paternak, my name is Kenneth Masters. I *do* work for the local authority, but I'm not here today in that capacity. May I come inside?"

The man looked wary, but Kenny had behaved professionally and it was obvious that he was one of the less dubious people who might visit. Moments later, his apprehensive expression refusing to fade as he opened the door wider, Paternak said, "Okay, then. Welcome to the old palace."

The property's interior was no worse than many Kenny had seen during his career so far. Junk filled the hallway, and in the lounge stood a tatty couch, a tattier armchair, a widescreen TV, a satellite box, a pile of what appeared to be import-only cigarettes, a case of scotch (one bottle open and no glass), and a carpet that looked as if it had last been vacuumed before a rowdy house party.

After Vincent Paternak, still looking sheepish, asked Kenny to sit down, the man slumped in the armchair and then resurrected a roll-up from the ashtray at his feet. "So what can I do you for, pal?"

Something about his phrase made Kenny feel uncomfortable. Once the man realised why he'd come, he might be less agreeable. Kenny took a moment to scrutinise Paternak, finding it hard to believe his partner had ever been attracted to him. But it was possible that the guy had once been appealing. Before corrosive lifestyle habits had taken grip, perhaps he'd even been a ladies' man. He was certainly cocky and spoke with a streetwise knowingness. Kenny knew his sort well; he'd gone to school with similar characters, who'd made his early life miserable.

"I've come to talk about Linda Bennett. I'm...well, I'm *with* her now. She has a son..." Kenny hesitated, considering the wisdom of going on, but then simply said it: "...a son she claims is *yours*."

This was the second time in as many days that he'd had to address the same difficult matter, and he wondered whether the man would be upset as Linda the previous night. Kenny watched Paternak register the information, eyes widening. But then he smirked in a way that actually put Kenny in mind of Duncan yesterday.

"Well, that's a turn up, eh?" Paternak dragged on his cigarette, which was almost down to the butt. Then he leaned forwards in his chair, clearly finding a defensive posture no longer necessary. "But I'm sorry to have to tell ya, pal, that you've been hoodwinked good n proper."

The guy's Yorkshire accent had a bluntness that caused Kenny to doubt himself. He'd arrived feeling confident but now felt compromised, as had happened often in the past. He didn't even get chance to reply before the man continued.

"Linda Bennett *had* every bloke in Leeds when she was a young un, mate. I admit that me n her went together for a while. But then I discovered her other interests, what she used to get up to with a bunch of weird fuckers whenever me back was turned. And you'd better believe it when I tell you that they made *me* look like Mary fucking Poppins."

Kenny eventually found his voice, but it was intrigue rather than anger that motivated his reply. "What do you mean?"

"What I *mean*, fella, is this: she n a bunch of

other sad sacks got involved with a guy well-known around these parts. This was about twenty years ago. Harry Topper, the fella was called. He described himself as some kind of..." The man paused, reached down to snatch up a bottle of scotch and swigged quickly from its neck. Finally, he added, "...some kind of *black magician*."

Kenny might have laughed if he hadn't felt so unsettled. He'd come across similarly bizarre accusations during his career, but never been personally involved in any. Linda having a promiscuous past had shocked him less than the associations to which his informant had alluded: *black magic*, had he said? Was he being serious?

Vincent Paternak swept a hand around the room. "Look around you, dude. Tell me what you see."

Kenny now felt even more confused. "I don't understand. What are you getting at?"

"Can you spot any family pictures on display? Any framed photos of kiddies on the mantelpiece?"

Nothing was on the mantelpiece; there wasn't really a mantelpiece, just a chipped shelf filled with grimy ornaments.

"Well, no. But what does that prove?"

"It proves, my friend, that I have *no children*. Christ, surely a glance at me confirms that I'm forty-going-on-death's-door. Don't you think that if I *could* have kids, I'd have had em by now?"

"I don't know." Just then, inspiration struck Kenny. "You don't *have* to have kids. I mean, I have none. Sometimes life just...well, it just goes that way."

"You must be referring to what that *bitch* has told you about my past. I suppose you – Mister Goody-Two-Shoes; man, I can smell *that* on you – I suppose you think that an ex-crackhead like me can't hold things together long enough to spawn a sprog or two. Is that it?" He laughed loudly and then stubbed out his butt in the highly populated ashtray. A moment later, he stood and clutched his groin with one clawed hand. "You're *wrong*, mate. *Sooo* wrong. The real reason I have no kids is because I *can't* have em. You hear me?"

When comprehension failed to register in Kenny's eyes, Vincent Paternak went bullishly on.

"I'm seedless, mate. A Jaffa. And if *she* tells you I'm the father of whatever little shit she's brought into this fucked-up world, then think again. There's about as much chance of me siring an heir to this glistenin' palace as you have of getting Linda fucking Bennett to play a straight game with ya." He came at Kenny, fists balled, but then turned for the lounge's exit. "Still, I wish you every luck with that, pal. Now kindly get the hell out of my gaff."

~7~

He'd driven north out of Leeds before he allowed himself to consider what he'd learned from Vincent Paternak. Darkness had now descended, moonlit shadows lurking in hedges alongside the roads. Following signs for Otley, a small town on the way to Skipton, he asked himself the question he'd suppressed until he'd put distance between himself and that man back in Leeds.

Why, when the guy had denied it, had Linda told him that Vincent Paternak was Duncan's father?

Kenny knew the man had good reasons to lie, mainly sixteen years of unpaid child maintenance. Kenny believed that Paternak had told the truth, however. Throughout his career, Kenny had heard every possible excuse from people attempting to evade their responsibilities, but the man had actually sounded convincing. Perhaps it was simply how he'd emasculated himself by confessing an inability to father children.

It wasn't easy for a man to admit to being inadequate in that way. Kenny always made a point of telling others that he'd chosen not to have children, mainly because he'd feel uncomfortable if they thought this decision was imposed by shortcomings. That was how men were. His father had constantly betrayed a similar masculine pride. Kenny recalled thinking how pathetic he'd considered this, but was he now resorting to something just as feeble?

Steering along a deserted country lane, Kenny sensed something shift nearby. He eased on the brakes, causing his headlamps to splash around in the unlit road. Phantom figures writhed among undergrowth standing to each side, but then his gaze was drawn to his rear-view mirror.

That was when he saw it.

The *figure* in the back of his car.

It looked as if it were made of chalk, despite being as large as him. Kenny, still gripping the steering wheel, slammed on the brakes, making tyres screech. This proved a fitting accompaniment to the *thing* now trying to poke its sorry excuse for a head between the two front seats.

It was his *dad's* face it bore, fashioned from the chalk-like substance that constituted the whole thing. The features were crude and rudimentary – wide forehead, deep-set eyes, narrow lips – but the figure's idiot sculptor had surely had Kenny's late father in mind.

"Desist while you can," hissed this chalk-man, spitting out clouds of dried white powder, its voice like a gust of wind down a dusty old chimney. Then its hands – boasting solid fingers, each pale and fragile – began tugging its jerry-built body forwards, as if eager to reach Kenny. *"You've been warned."*

Terror assaulted Kenny like a punch to the guts. He felt his bladder slacken like that of a frightened boy. Horror stole in, robbing him of logic, forcing him to stall the car engine.

Moments later, he wrestled for the door-handle, fighting to escape the *thing* now stretching for him. After removing his gaze from the rear-view mirror, he twisted to look directly at the imposter gradually squeezing its unstable frame into the front of the car.

Kenny's vision now unmediated by glass, the figure lost some of its desiccated appearance. The slipshod body now appeared moist, as if a single touch would expose a dampish material from which it was constructed like an ancient mummy, either papier-mâché or moulded pulp. Although its body resembled little more than a mass of whitish gunge, the leering face, alive and alert, drew Kenny's full attention, eliciting both confusion and dread. His dad had died five years ago, but suddenly it felt like looking at him again. This entity was surely an unfinished model, some black magician's trick.

With a fearful act of defiance, Kenny finally struggled free of the car. His whole body shook and shook, no more cohesive than water. Despite registering aspects of the world around him – the solid road, breeze-blown foliage, a pitch-black sky littered with stars – he was unable to process further thoughts until he'd scrambled away from the vehicle. Then he turned to see whether the creature was in pursuit.

Light in the area was poor, just a faint glow from his unextinguished headlamps, but Kenny immediately noticed that nobody – or rather, no*thing* – had followed him out of the car. Edging steadily closer, heart hammering under his ribs, he observed that the interior was now empty.

A hallucination; it must have been. Strain from his challenging week – a heavy workload at the office, so many domestic tensions at home – had at last caught up with him. That was all this was. That was all it could be.

He *really* wanted to believe this. But how could he?

After leaning tentatively back inside the car, he noticed whitish streaks of a powder smeared down the backs of his front seats. These were finger-marks, and although their maker had now vanished, the dry-moist runnels no longer allowed Kenny the luxury of self-deception.

~8~

The moment he got home, Kenny went straight

upstairs to tackle the boy and his mother. Duncan wasn't there, however, neither in his bedroom nor anywhere else in the house. But after entering the master bedroom, Kenny saw Linda lying awake in bed, sheets clutched about her as if protectively. She looked wired, eyes staring. Then, her voice cautious, she said, "Hi. Where've you been? It's gone six o'clock."

Ever reliable, he was usually home by half-past-five; Linda had clearly realised that something had delayed him. He hadn't understood how closely she monitored his activities. It wasn't as if she bothered much with her son.

"Who's Harry Topper?" he asked, his voice involuntarily firm.

If she'd looked furious yesterday when he'd made his enquiries, she now appeared shocked. She was unable to speak for several seconds, after which Kenny explained where he'd been that afternoon and what he'd been told. He omitted the events in the car, however; he was still trying to come to terms with such a mind-rupturing experience.

Once Kenny had finished, Linda said, "We were young, Kenny. We were all very confused."

"That doesn't answer my question, Linda."

"I'm trying to. Just give me a moment." She rubbed her face with the heels of both hands and then returned her gaze to him. "I have only vague recollections about what went on at his house. We were always on drugs. But...but he offered us satisfaction. *Closure*. I mean, he had the ability to make us feel *something*."

"Are you talking about Topper?"

"Yes."

Kenny sat on the bed, but refused to embrace Linda at this stage. He had other questions about what the man had been up to – hadn't Vincent Paternak mentioned black magic? Hadn't Kenny experienced something related to that only hours ago? – but felt scared about doing so right now. Instead he asked, "So who *was* Duncan's father?"

Linda dropped her head. "I'm sorry I misled you. I thought you just wanted the information – you know, to satisfy your curiosity. I didn't think you'd actually visit him."

"But I told you why. I'm concerned about Dunc'."

"He's *sixteen*, Kenny. A young man now. He doesn't need us looking out for him." She paused, as if considering the wisdom of adding more, but then did so. "Remember what you were like at that age. Did your dad hassle you that way? Did you want to remain under your parents' thumbs forever?"

Linda knew that these were tricky questions for him, because he'd discussed his awkward upbringing with her previously. They also summoned to Kenny's mind images of that *thing* he'd witnessed in his car. The truth was that, even as a teenager, he'd never caused his mum and dad any concern. He'd been well-behaved, respectful, and thoughtful. But had this left him unnecessarily fretful about youngsters who weren't as reserved and vulnerable? Basically, did Kenny have unfinished business from his past, arising from a strained relationship with two people who'd overprotected him?

He looked up, eyes suddenly fierce. "This has nothing to do with me. It's about Dunc'. Now, are you going to tell me what I need to know?"

Linda visibly shrunk from his tone, her head falling to one side. "I can't, Kenny. I just *can't.*"

Did she even know who Duncan's father was? That made Kenny so angry that he had to stand at once from the bed. Then, watching her until he was convinced that she wasn't about to add more, he got up and left the room before saying anything he might regret later.

There was one other thing he could try. After thumping downstairs, he grabbed the telephone and dialled a number from memory. The line rang and rang, but Kenny knew the man would be there. A good journalist was always on duty, and as Kenny shoved aside the curtains to glance across the moonlit housing estate, the call eventually connected.

"Hi. Stephen Bask here. Have you got news for me?"

Despite his mood, Kenny couldn't help smiling at the way his acquaintance always answered the phone. They'd met ten years earlier, when Kenny had been naive enough to believe that the media had influence over national policy development. Bask had sought a contact in the local authority and Kenny had agreed to help, hoping his idealistic views would benefit from a larger audience than regional steering groups and funding focused committees. It had amounted to little for either party, but the two men had got along well. Kenny recalled that Bask still owed him at least one favour.

Kenny got down to business at once, asking Bask for the information he required. After consulting a few files, the journalist was able to furnish him with all he needed. Then Kenny hung up and grabbed his car keys, before heading outside to start his vehicle.

He now understood why the figure warning him off earlier – not his actual dad, but some supernatural facsimile of the man – had appeared on the fringes of Otley: this was the town in which, according to Bask, Harry Topper had once lived. Kenny was also convinced that it would be where he'd find Duncan this evening. Kenny typed the residential address the journalist had given him into his satnav and started driving.

The scandal had occurred fifteen years earlier. Kenny would have been eight years old at the time, and although reports had referred to underage participants involved in orgies and dubious rituals, he'd been unaware of references in the local news. These events had resulted in the conviction of a number of youngsters on charges of cruelty to animals. That was the only prosecution police had managed to make, because the practice of magic rituals, however deviant in intention, wasn't actually illegal. Harry Topper had received a suspended sentence after killing a cat and several chickens. Other participants, Linda presumably among them, had been given cautions and advised never to regroup.

Topper had since disappeared, or at least refrained from activities that attracted the law's attention. Rumours suggested that he'd taken his interests underground, but that was all that was known about him...except for what Stephen Bask, while researching to write an exposé of Topper, had learned about his childhood. That was when the truly bad stuff had emerged.

Kenny's thoughts were interrupted as his satnav reported him close to his destination. He'd steered along deserted roads, each twisting and turning as his car headed through countryside. There was little property in this area, and Kenny doubted it was served by bus routes, which made him wonder how Duncan had travelled here after school. Kenny had little doubt that this was where the boy visited each evening. Whether he'd been approached by Topper – a frightening thought, given what

Kenny now knew about the man – or Duncan had made first contact, it must be true that the boy had sought his father in the dark house that had just appeared up ahead.

~9~

When Harry Topper was twelve years old, his father had burned off his genitals with a bunsen burner. The older man had been a scientist, living and conducting experiments in this old house near Otley. His family, a son and a wife, had always suffered from his volatile temperament. It was unclear whether the elder Topper had committed such a terrible act of surgery on his only child in a typical rage or as a botched attempt to...well, the journalist was unable to speculate about his nefarious purpose. Bask had nonetheless claimed that Topper's father's research had gone beyond what was, by anyone's standards, ethically acceptable and ventured into shocking territory.

Despite his naivety in some matters, Kenny had seen a lot of the world and was less shaken by what he'd learnt about the Toppers than others might be. Determination now lending him courage, he parked at the roadside and then climbed out of his car, trying not to glance at any chalky streaks remaining inside the vehicle.

The property was a two-storey detached set in generous grounds. The gardens were run-to-seed unruly, and Kenny refused to speculate about what might lurk among hedges, gnarled trees, and emaciated plants. Returning his attention to the front entrance as he approached, he noticed a gap alongside its frame: the door was unlocked. He paced bullishly forwards, hearing the house welcome his arrival with a series of hollow echoes.

His mobile phone's flashlight helped him to explore the ground floor. There were four rooms – lounge, dining room, kitchen, and a utility area – but, other than sticks of insect-ridden furniture, all were empty. Next, he climbed a rickety flight of steps and found the same on the first floor: three bedrooms, a large bathroom, and a room that might once have been a study to judge by pictures of astral bodies still clinging to its walls. But the level was otherwise deserted.

As he turned to retreat downstairs, Kenny spotted a figure shift far along the corridor, whitish and blurred. His heart nearly stopped in his chest. But, after steadying himself by slumping against one wall, he recognised this shape for what it was: his reflection in a mirror hanging askew opposite the landing. Reeling with undiminished unease, he rushed back down the flight, eager to flee this creepy place. He sensed something deeply unpleasant about the building, as if terrible past events had been stored inside it and weren't entirely extinguished.

If the house really was occupied, where could Duncan be? Perhaps there was an outhouse in the property's grounds. Kenny, hands still shaking, felt more than keen to go outside and look. Indeed, he'd taken several paces towards the way out when he hesitated a moment, swinging his phone back along the downstairs corridor. That was when he spotted a doorway that must give on to a cellar.

He knew he should have considered this possibility first. Whatever activities still occurred here would surely remain out of view of passers-by. As Kenny headed for the lower level, he wondered how Topper had originally attracted Duncan from afar. Perhaps some kind of magic had summoned the boy, the natural bond that existed between fathers and sons. Kenny's own dad, rendered chalky and terrifying, had tried preventing him from visiting the place, but Kenny reckoned that must have been a test, and one he'd passed. He was now ready to tackle the next stage and would do so by taking on a responsibility to which previously he'd only half-committed himself: being a father of sorts to Duncan. Perhaps the boy had even sensed Kenny's previous reticence, like a knife to the guts. But Kenny would put an end to this. By conquering the child inside himself, Kenny could become a real father.

He grabbed the cellar's rusted handle and pulled open the door.

~10~

The steps leading into the cellar felt like ice through Kenny's shoes. The immediate space up ahead was as black as a power failure, but he hoisted his phone again, revealing the wall to one side. He might have thought it was moving if he hadn't realised how badly his hands still shook.

After reaching the bottom of the stairs, he moved the phone left and then right, attempting to illuminate the cellar. The flashlight beam was challenged by a darkness so thick it resembled churning oil. He inhaled cool air that seemed full of dust. An aroma of rotting debris struck his nostrils, but could he also detect a *human* odour? If that was the case, he'd have to venture farther to discover its source. Drawing a sharp breath, he began pacing across the floor.

Objects hindered his shuffling feet. One large chunk – was this made of wood or metal? – threatened to topple him, but Kenny managed to maintain his balance. Concern about falling was actually less troubling than arousing whatever denizens made this place their home. But surely he was being foolish. Other than so much junk, nothing else was here. It was dispiriting to reflect that the farther he moved, the less likely it seemed he'd chance upon a clue as to his stepson's whereabouts.

Just then, however, the room started glowing with a weird light; this soon rendered Kenny's phone unnecessary. He pushed it into one pocket and then looked around at the newly illuminated cellar, gasping at what he saw. Surely the room's size exceeded that of the house above. This underground chamber lacked the property's squareness, possessing a circular form whose perimeter walls were tens of yards apart. Kenny observed these dimensions peripherally, because suddenly he was captivated by what he noticed lurking at the heart of the expansive cellar.

Twelve children – of varying ages, and all boys – stood up against a large organic growth. Most had their lips clamped around several of this thing's leaking appendages, multiple outcroppings reaching from its trunk-like body. The growth was neither a tree nor any plant Kenny recognised. About ten feet high and almost reaching the cellar's ceiling, its trunk was about four feet thick. He couldn't tell whether it was dark grey or deep green, but Kenny felt reluctant to move any closer. All he could do was continue to observe what the dozen boys appeared to be doing.

Were they actually *drinking* from the treelike thing? Each of them appeared to derive some form of sustenance, their faces, clamped to nipple-like saplings, looking contented and soporific, like those of drug addicts after a fix or babies while breastfeeding. Moments later, one of the boys, surely no older than thirteen, detached himself from his companions.

Kenny watched him cross the cellar, following at a sensible distance and trying not to alert the others. Once Kenny had paced several yards, the cellar's light picked out an oblong patch of darkness which, upon closer analysis, turned out to be a tall opening in the curved wall. It was a doorway, and then the boy, still boasting a drugged demeanour, stepped promptly through it. Without reflecting on any consequences, Kenny quickly followed.

Now it was too dark to see anything at all. A chill draught assaulted him, combated only when he sunk lower in his jacket. The scent remained earthy and acrid, but could he now detect the odour of some kind of dairy product? Kenny recalled the boys sucking the glands of that hideous tree-thing, like infants consuming mother's milk. But none of these reflections was helpful. He moved immediately forwards, headed towards a noise he'd just heard. It sounded as if something nearby was being repeatedly struck.

After reaching a solid barrier, Kenny stretched out to grab what were surely iron bars. These ran vertical, were spaced evenly apart, and, after moving his hands from left to right, he counted eight of them. Beyond stood a cold stretch of wall, and then almost certainly more bars. Now realising that he must be in a room full of caged doorways, he squinted his eyes to adjust his vision.

More of that weird light picked out the small room beyond the bars directly ahead. At its heart was a figure seated on a stool, perched like a mannequin in a commercial shop window. If not for its intermittent movement, Kenny might have mistaken it for a lifeless dummy. But the closer he observed this thing, the more it resembled what he'd actually expected: another of the chalk-moist creatures to which he'd been introduced earlier that day.

This one held a person: a small boy, maybe five or six years old, draped across its lap, head hanging over one side, and legs the other. His bottom was exposed at the top of his arched form, while the whitish figure with uncertain features – twitching face, limbs staccato in movement – repeatedly spanked the boy, producing the noise Kenny had heard earlier. The chalk-man, surely a facsimile of this boy's absent father, was exercising the discipline he surely required.

Each strike appeared jerky, like stop-motion animation broadcast at only a few frames per second. The faint light lent the act a spectral animation. The powdery figure's face betrayed a combination of grim and yet benevolent features: raging eyes, narrow nose, thick lips clenched with punitive resolve. The fake person looked troubled by his actions, but its repeated assaults were nonetheless essential; Kenny knew that well. Then he moved along to the next cell.

This one contained an older boy, maybe ten or eleven, tightly hugging another of those wet-dry chalk-men. The expression the latest figure conceded was vacant and yet loving, like that of a man asked to reveal his true feelings without first consuming alcohol. All the same, the boy it held in slack, powdery arms looked unconcerned by his pseudo-father's half-heartedness; it seemed to be enough that he was here at all. Irrepressibly tearful, the boy kept hold of the figure, grasping and grasping its flaking form. Every few seconds, with something like docile obedience, the chalk-father patted the boy on the head, as if acknowledging his existence, putting him right in this world of woes.

Kenny turned away, moisture marring his vision, and finally moved to the next room. All the while, he struggled to control involuntary reflections on his own father. Discipline and affection, the two acts he'd seen dramatized in the cells so far, would have served Kenny well as a child; intuition told him this was true. He recalled all the unrest of his teenage years, his nature suppressed by timidity and parental concerns about offending others.

That was no problem for Duncan, however.

Kenny knew he'd find his stepson in the last cell here, a corridor offshoot from the dope-shop that was the house's cellar. That treelike growth at that circular room's heart offered fatherless boys succour before they engaged in a sequence of rough treatments conveying them from discipline and then to love and finally to triumph over paternal influence.

Duncan stood over the pulp-like body of his facsimile father. Perhaps the man who'd sired him had once attended Harry Topper's orgies, dabbling with others in forms of black magic which involved killing animals along with other decadent acts. Linda's pregnancy might have been an accident, her claim not to know who her son's father even genuine. But Harry Topper must have known. Wherever the man now resided, he knew a great deal and drew on such knowledge to help Duncan and many like him, fatherless boys with nobody to guide them, to offer them strength, and then to be overpowered.

As these thoughts raced through Kenny's mind, Duncan brought down a baseball bat on his pretend-dad's face.

The prostrate figure's head collapsed, principally because it was made of nothing firmer than papier-mâché. After more blows which caved in the skull, the boy started on its legs. Each buckled and broke with a sickening sound, like branches snapped over a brutal lumberjack's knee. The torso came next, and then the arms, and before long the figure's body was reduced to chalky residue. Duncan stamped on the remains, grinding almost-bones and faux flesh underfoot until all was little more than whitish stains on the floor.

Kenny intuitively understood what had happened here. Once the boy was done, Kenny called to his stepson through the cage's bars.

"It's over, Dunc'," he said, his voice packed with involuntary tenderness. "Come out of there. Let me take you home."

The boy – or rather, young man now – turned to look, revealing a face full of hope, fight, and determination. Dropping the bat, he began moving, raising a hand to the barred entrance and then giving it a tug. The door creaked promptly open, delighting Kenny.

Less concealed now by shadow, Duncan smiled and said, "Thanks for coming for me. It's…it's not nice here. But I *had* to do it."

An image of his own ineffectual father flashed suddenly in Kenny's mind, but was then gone, a mild epidemic succumbing to some powerful antidote.

"I understand," he said, and then put an arm around Duncan, around his stepson, whom he'd support with love forevermore.

Also by Gary Fry:

Novels

The House of Canted Steps (PS Publishing, 2010)
Fearful Festivities (Screaming Dreams, 2011)
Conjure House (DarkFuse, 2013)
Severed (DarkFuse, 2014)
Siren of Depravity (DarkFuse, 2016)

Novellas & Novelettes

The Invisible Architect of Psychopathy (in *Feral Companions*, Pendragon Press, 2010)
Abolisher of Roses (Spectral Press, 2011)
The Respectable Face of Tyranny (Spectral Press, 2012)
Emergence (DarkFuse, 2013)
Lurker (DarkFuse, 2013)
Menace (DarkFuse, 2014)
Savage (DarkFuse, 2014)
Mutator (DarkFuse, 2014)
What They Find in the Woods (Dark Minds Press, 2016)
Scourge (Snowbooks, 2016)
The Doom That Came to Whitby Town (Gray Friar Press, 2016)
The Rage of Cthulhu (Horrific Tales, 2017)

Collections

The Impelled and Other Head Trips (Crowswing
Books, 2006)

World Wide Web and Other Lovecraftian Upgrades
(Humdrumming Books, 2007)

*Sanity and Other Delusions: Tales of Psychological
Horror* (PS Publishing, 2007)

Mindful of Phantoms (Gray Friar Press, 2009)

Shades of Nothingness (PS Publishing, 2013)

Visit Gary Fry at his website:
gary-fry.com

Shadows 9 – Winter Freits
by Andrew David Barker

Shadows 10 – The Dead
by Paul Kane

Shadows 11 – The Forest of Dead Children
by Andrew Hook

Shadows 12 – At Home in the Shadows
by Gary McMahon

blackshuckbooks.co.uk/shadows